SEA HUNTERS: SHONISAURUS

BY

WILLIAM MEIKLE

SEVEREDPRESS

SEA HUNTERS: SHONISAURUS

WWW.SEVEREDPRESS.COM

This novel is a work of fiction. Names, characters, places and incidents are the product of the author's imagination, or are used fictitiously. Any resemblance to actual events, locales or persons, living or dead, is purely coincidental.

ISBN: 978-1-922861-23-8

-1-

"So how did you come to leave the Royal Navy, Mr. Seton?"

It had taken less than a minute for me to know I didn't like the man…the potential client… who was sitting across the desk. If he had 'officious wee wanker' tattooed on his forehead it wouldn't have told me anything I didn't know already. I had so far suffered the third degree about my boat, my crew, and my last two jobs, the urge to tell the man to fuck off was reaching boiling point, and now I was expected to dredge up the worst night of my life to satisfy his curiosity?

As my auld grandad would have said… fuck, no.

"We had a difference of opinion," I replied and put a smile on it to show I was sincere.

"Care to elaborate?"

"No."

The word lay between us across the table, and for a second I thought it was going to blow the whole deal. When he didn't pick me up on it, I knew my services were the most important thing; the interview was no more than an arse-covering measure in case it all went tits up later. For the first time since I entered the room I began to relax.

"Look," I said, "You know my rates, you know my record. You've obviously spoken to other people I've worked with so you know I'm reliable. I can get the job done, but before I can give you any assurances on that score, I'll need to know what the job is."

It had been a hectic day already. *The Havenhome* was moored in Hong Kong when the request for an interview came in and rather than hunt up the crew who were currently enjoying some hard-earned shore leave, I chartered a plane, island hopping down to Manilla. Now I was sitting in the Subic Bay Yacht Club, almost lost in a deep armchair, with a view overlooking a sun-dazzled marina packed full of yachts I'd never be able to afford, owned by people I would never understand. The golden people were at play and here I was auditioning to be their help. It irked me somewhere down in my old-school Scottish socialist roots, but I'd long ago learned to push that away when it came to the job at hand; my dreams meant I needed the money.

I was also wool-gathering when I should be listening. I dragged my gaze from the boats outside and focussed on my interviewer.

The man in the chair opposite, David Franks, had introduced himself as the General Manager. It certainly looked like it paid well, given the cut of his jib and the heavy gold watch he made sure I noticed.

He sat in a chair deliberately several inches larger than the one I occupied and ruled his antique mahogany desk like a king of old. He obviously fit right in here among the opulence and, equally obviously, found the need for my services to be beneath him. I guessed something was costing the club money; being hit, hard, in the pocket was the only thing that bothered pricks like Franks. My hunch was proved right seconds later.

"We've been losing yachts in the area," Franks said.

"I'd noticed," I replied. "People too. How many are you up to now?"

"Three."

"Yachts or people?"

"Both."

I got the impression he considered the yachts to be the bigger loss of the two, and he confirmed it soon enough.

"One of our Russian friends has lost a fifty million dollar asset," he said.

"I thought he picked her up in London for fifty quid and a bottle of Bollinger," I replied, but he wasn't rising to the bait. He went on to describe the 'accident' but I'd already read about it in the papers and had access to some of the more unpublishable lurid photos through a friend in Fleet Street.

It had been only twenty miles from where we sat; the girl had gone swimming off the stern of the yacht… and gone missing. What they found floating behind them a few minutes later was too small and in too many bits to identify; the Russian said later he'd recognised an earring, still attached to an ear that wasn't attached to anything else. While they were scooping what was left of her out of the water, something hit the yacht, hard, from below. The story was that they'd been preoccupied with the 'rescue' and hadn't seen a rock, but I'd seen the photos of the hull as it lay on the bottom; it looked like it had been chewed.

As for the Russian, his crew had been well prepped, the lifeboat did its job, and he lived to make his insurance claim; he was already back in London, probably with another fifty quid and bottle of champagne at the ready for any takers.

That 'accident' was the most newsworthy of the three, but one of the others, to my mind at least, was far more interesting. It had happened in the sunken caldera of an ancient volcano forty miles northwest of Manilla. A pair of Australian divers, looking for wrecks, had found something they didn't bargain for. It was their description of the thing that ate their boat that interested me. They described it as 'something like a big croc. But paler, toothier and definitely a lot bigger. This fucker was huge.'

That description was the main reason I was now prepared to put up with the wee shitebag opposite me in the office. That, and also the main reason why

I left the Royal Navy, although I wasn't about to speak about either. I stayed quiet and let him stew a bit. You could almost see the bean counter working behind his eyes. I must have come down on the right side of the equation. He tugged at the cuffs of his shirt, looked down his nose at me one last time, and nodded.

"We agree to your terms," he said. "You have a week. If it's not done by then, I'll get somebody else."

"It might take longer…"

"It can't. High season starts first of the month. We're going to have more millionaires per square mile here than anywhere else on the planet. We need them to trust us with their safety."

His use of the royal 'we' was really getting on my tits, and it was long past time I had a smoke, so I stood up and reached over a hand to shake on the deal. At first, I thought he wasn't going to accept it, then he slid a cold, almost slimy palm into mine and gave me the barest modicum of a limp shake; it felt like touching a newly caught trout.

"We will need daily reports; twice a day in fact."

I didn't shake on that; I wasn't going to agree to anything I had no intention of doing.

"I'll be in touch," I said and left him there staring out over the marina, the bean counter tallying up the value of the assets laid out below him. I went out onto the main boardwalk, leaned on a rail, lit a cigarette and stared out over the same assets. I wasn't seeing the beans. I was seeing the path that had led me to this spot.

I'm John Seton. In case you haven't guessed already, I'm Scottish; a heavyset, heavy-bearded, taciturn bastard with a heart of gold, at least that's what the crew tell me, when they're talking to me. I grew up in a fishing village up near Aberdeen, spent my youth at sea, my later youth in a series of bars, and my young manhood in the Royal Navy, mainly on the North Atlantic runs keeping an eye on the Russian fleet. I mostly enjoyed those years, moving up the ranks, getting as far as Lieutenant before the night everything changed… but I don't talk about that unless I'm drunk.

Let's just say the Navy and I parted company, none too amicably. After that I tried big-game fishing for a time, taking rich Yanks looking for marlin, but that quickly lost its appeal. You see, I'd developed an itch I couldn't scratch.

Fate gave me a kick in the arse as I was bumming my way around the Bahamas taking deck jobs wherever I could find them. I heard of a boat for sale, a boat that would allow me to pursue my dreams. Three months and a bank loan I couldn't afford later I took delivery of *The Havenhome* and my path was set. I found some crew, some other crew found me, and we set about building a reputation. Over the last few years we've become pretty good at it.

What do we do?

We hunt sea monsters for people that don't believe in sea monsters.

Other boat captains call me Ahab behind my back. I don't talk about that either, even when I'm drunk.

- 2 -

The Havenhome began life in the late Sixties as a Storm-class patrol boat for the Norwegian Navy. She got pensioned off to the Latvian Navy where she settled into old age and finally came to me through a dealer in the Baltic, no questions asked. She's a hundred and twenty feet long, twenty across the beam with a six-foot draught and, with the modifications we've made in the past few years, she's fast, agile, and the perfect vessel for the job we need her to do. She's also home, the first real one I've had in years, and if anyone wants to talk shite about her, they've got me to answer to.

I'd made some calls from Manilla Airport so by the time I got back to the dock in Hong Kong the crew had been rounded up, herded aboard and set about readying for departure. I had McCallum to thank for that; Geordie McCallum, First Mate, best friend, drinking partner and watcher of my back from the Navy days. He's a wee wiry whippet of a man, five foot six and ten stone sopping wet, Glaswegian printed through every pore of him like on a stick of rock, mild-mannered in the main, but with a temper that can strip paint off the bulkheads when riled. He was waiting in my cabin at the rear of the boat when I got aboard.

"So what's it to be this time, Johnnie Boy?" he said. "Is it a strange beastie, or just another shark hunt?"

"It's a beastie all right," I said, heading for the whisky bottle. "Might even be The Beastie; the description fits."

"Come on, lad. We both ken that's unlikely."

"What's unlikely is that yon thing exists in the first place."

"Aye, you're right enough there," he replied, and took a whisky when offered, savoring it before going on. "So, Manilla, is it? That's a new one for me. Is yon yacht club as posh as it looks in the brochures?"

"Posher. And with more wankers per square mile than Belgravia on a Saturday night."

"So why are they slumming it by hiring the likes of us? Surely they've got the local Navy in their pocket?"

"Probably, but that wouldn't look good in yon brochures you just mentioned. With us they get plausible deniability if we fuck up."

It took two days of the week I'd been given just to get back to the area from Hong Kong, two days in which the crew bitched about everything from their canceled shore leave to the shitty weather that was blowing through; well everybody except Ruru, our harpoonist. He only talks when there's a beast to be taken down or when he's angry, and I've only seen him angry once. I don't want to see it again.

As for me, I spent most of the time on the bridge, drinking coffee laced with rum and smoking too many high-tar cigarettes, trying not to get ahead of myself on the job to come. Moira, my helmsman, kept me grounded. I'd found her in Ireland; she was bored cruising between Larne and Stranrear on the car ferry, and looking for wider horizons. I'd offered her a job heading down to the Azores and she was still with me five years later. She was having an on/off relationship with Geordie, currently off, and she kept me amused with a litany of Geordie's failures, of which, she assured me, there were many. I'd decided the best place for us to start our search was at the caldera where the Australians had got into trouble. By the time we arrived I knew more about Geordie's sex life than he did. The talking had done its job though, and Moira's mood had improved along with the weather as we dropped anchor.

It certainly was a spectacular site. At some point in antiquity the volcano had blown and sunk from the inside, leaving a mile-wide ring of black jagged peaks as witness. There was only one entry into the resultant circle, not much wider than *The Havenhome*, and once inside it felt like we had left the real world behind and entered a silent, calm paradise all to ourselves. The sea lay like a thin cover of water over a sheet of blue glass and the sun blazed down on us from a cloudless sky.

It was time to start earning our fee.

I went out on deck and found that O'Shea had already second guessed me and was getting an AUV ready for delivery. He's another one I found in Ireland. He'd only been with us a couple of months, but I already knew that if there was a better engineer in the business, I'd yet to meet them.

"What do you think, Cap," he said, not looking up from the small bot's control panel. "Twenty feet deep, and a half-mile wide circle do for you?"

The five-foot long AUV could be programmed to make just about any journey and would keep sending telemetry back to us for as long as its battery held out. It was equipped with an acoustic hydrophone and sensors to monitor water temperature, salinity and current. It was the hydrophone reading I was particularly interested in.

"Get her in the water, lad. The sooner we find this beastie the sooner we get paid."

"And the sooner I get back to the warm lass I left in Hong Kong."

I ignored that; I knew from experience O'Shea was more than willing to discuss his sex life in great detail, and I was still carrying mental pictures of Geordie and Moira in my head; there's some things about the crew a captain just doesn't need to know.

"Once you've got the bot in the water, we'll circle round and drop some of the other wee buoys on the perimeter."

We used small buoys with attached hydrophones to supplement the bot and allow us to triangulate the position of any beast that might be making some noise in the deeps. We even had a cunning bit of software that could immediately identify particular species, if they existed on the database. The technology had worked well for us on previous jobs and, given the enclosed nature of this current site, I had high hopes for it here.

But after we got the bots running there was nothing doing for the rest of the day. The waters below seemed devoid of any life at all, at least any that was making any sound. Temperature and salinity readings barely fluctuated from what I'd class as average in the circumstances, and the boat was heating up fast with every hour that passed. The crew's tempers rose concurrently.

There are arguments and there are arguments. The one that got my attention was coming from the galley and sounded like it was more serious than usual. I got there to find O'Shea backed in a corner by an angry cook wielding a cleaver. I wasn't too willing to intervene; Stevie Watts knew her way around blades, both kitchen and fighting, with far too much efficiency for it to be safe to be around her when she was riled. And she looked to be more than riled; she looked furious. When she saw me and turned to speak, her South London accent came through strong; that's when I knew she was serious.

"You tell this asshole to keep his hands to himself, Boss, or you'll be finding his balls in the stew at supper."

I'd found Stevie in a bar in Lewisham one dark night of the soul a few years back. I was the only white person present; being a traveling man by nature I hadn't really considered it a problem, but two young local lads, neither any older than eighteen, decided to make something of it. Stevie came out of the kitchen, assessed the situation in seconds, and had the lads fucking off just as quickly. She smiled at me, I smiled back and we shared a bunk for two months before we both realized we made better friends than lovers. I thought she might have left then, but she enjoyed the life and she cooked like an angel.

Right now, she looked more like a demon.

The Irishman attempted to charm his way out of it. He smiled and flashed his eyes.

"I was just being friendly."

I guessed it usually got him plenty of action with the young lassies he was used to, but Stevie and I both knew that was the wrong move. O'Shea didn't realize how much trouble he, or rather his bollocks, were in. Stevie doesn't go in much for kidding about. I knew that. He didn't. But he was about to find out.

I had just resolved that I was, reluctantly, going to have to step in, when fate saved us all from fucking up.

The boat took a sudden lurch to port and I was thrown against Stevie; luckily she was fast enough to move the cleaver out of harm's way, otherwise it might have been my balls in the stew. Dishes rattled, pans clattered, O'Shea made a remarkable one handed save to stop a bottle of Vodka from hitting the floor, and I just about managed to keep my hands off Stevie.

"What the fuck was that?" Stevie said.

It was wee Geordie who answered, his shout ringing out from above us on the deck.

"Found the fucker."

- 3 -

I was second on deck; Ruru was always first whenever there was any action and he was already heading for the harpoon mounting. But there was nothing for him to take aim at. The boat settled quickly back onto an even keel and soon there was only a slight rocking to show for the fact that we'd been hit at all… that and a swirl in the water to port that was also soon dissipated, leaving the flat calm behind once more.

"There's no damage below, but I wouldn't like us to take too many more punches like that," O'Shea said from behind me. "What the hell was it? Did anybody see the fucker?"

Nobody answered until Geordie popped his head out of the bridge.

"Didna see it, lad," he said to me. "But we've caught something on the computers. And whatever it is, it's fucking huge."

For once Geordie hadn't been exaggerating. We had the whole crew huddled round the screens a few minutes later. We were all used to the kinds of images we could get from the likes of shoals of fish or even whales, but this was something else; it seemed to be about two thirds as big as *The*

Havenhome, and moving faster than anything that size had a right to be moving. And it cried out as it came, or at least that's what the hydrophones sounded like, a high, mournful echoing wail that doppIered towards, then away from us. I couldn't be exactly sure, but it was my guess we'd got a glancing blow from its tail fluke as it went underneath us.

"Just a wee tickle," O'Shea said.

"Yes," Stevie said at his back, "And look what happened when you tried that with me."

I shushed them to silence and, thankfully, it appeared that Stevie's temper was forgotten in light of the beast's arrival in our vicinity. I shooed everyone but Geordie and Moira out onto deck to keep an eye out for its return. We watched the screens and listened to the hydrophones, but wherever it was, it had gone quiet again.

"Silent and deadly, just like wan o' your farts," Geordie said.

"I think it's him," I said, more to myself than in any attempt at conversation, but I was answered from behind us.

"I think it's about time you told me about your white whale," O'Shea said.

"Not going to happen," I replied.

Geordie looked at me.

"He has a right to know; he's the only wan who disnae."

I was still loath to comply but I saw Geordie's point. All for one and one for all and all that happy crappy. But I definitely couldn't do it sober.

"In that case, I'll be needing a drink," I said.

"So will I," Geordie answered.

I left Moira in charge of the bridge with orders not to disturb us unless the beastie returned and retired to my cabin with Geordie, O'Shea and a bottle of Scotch; it was the third of those with which I was intending to get most familiar.

Even settled in my own cabin with my things around me, a stiff drink at hand and a smoke in the other, I still found I couldn't start, so Geordie filled O'Shea in on how it began while I let the memories into the place I'd banished them from years ago.

"It was a filthy night," he began. "Your man here was First Lieutenant, I was First Mate, and the Navy, in their wisdom, had left us in charge of their boat for the night shift. She was Destroyer class, 30 feet longer than *The Havenhome* but with two hundred crew aboard, if you can imagine that. We'd spent six months in the far North Atlantic, freezing our bollocks off looking for Russians who were freezing their bollocks off looking for us. Neither of us found fuck all. We liked the night shift well enough though; we got some time to ourselves and we could have a smoke up on deck with naebody shouting at us. Normally it was a cushy number. But that night, something found us."

And just like that the memories kicked in. I was drinking Scotch, smoking a cigarette, and talking, but all of that was happening somewhere else, overpowered by scenes that still ran in my head with all the vividness of a big-screen movie experience despite the intervening years.

I'm standing on the upper deck above the bridge, rain lashing in my face, cupping a cigarette in my palm against the wind. I'm out here because we've picked up a ping on the radar, something in these waters with us that shouldn't be here, something that has already circled us once and is now spiraling in closer. I have no idea what the fuck it is, although the word 'submarine' keeps popping to mind.

All I know is that it's big and fast but I don't want to wake the captain if it's just a curious fin whale, so here I am, peering into the night in the dark like a fucking idiot when I should have been calling for battle stations. I can't see a thing, just black sea and driving rain.

The first hit comes on the starboard side while I'm looking to port, a jolt so hard it throws me off my feet and almost tosses me over the side. My first thought is torpedo, my second thought is that we're fucked, and my third thought is that maybe I should go wake the captain. But when the second hit comes there's no time for anything. The boat lurches sickeningly underfoot, and suddenly feels heavier; it's not something you can describe if you haven't experienced it yourself, but I know we are holed under the waterline and are taking in water.

Sirens blare.

Geordie has raised the alarm and the crew are waking up to flooding on the lower decks. I'm trying desperately to find someone, anyone, to help me get lifeboats in the water, and the boat is floundering fast beneath my feet.

And that's when I turn my head at just the right moment and I see it. It's coming right at us, the size of a bus and from a head-on view it appears to be all teeth with two almost-black eyes, the leftmost of which is underscored by a long white scar that runs from the eye to the upper lip of its long jaw. It's no whale, of that I'm sure, but quite what it might be is beyond my explanation at that point because I only have two seconds before it hits us again, hard, amid-ships, and my world tumbles arse-over-tit.

Next thing I know I'm underwater and trying to swallow most of it. I manage to get to the surface only after shucking off my overcoat and thrashing about for what seems like an eternity. I come up, suck air, and only then am I aware that the night is full of screams. I'm just in time to see the boat's stern go down, the bow go up and the whole fucking thing vanishes in a bubble of foam and steam. I see a lifeboat, head for it and am within twenty feet of reaching welcoming hands when a gargantuan head comes out of the waves, mouth agape and swallows any hope of rescue in one mouthful. As the beast bites down, I see men and boat and oars all mashed into fragments before it swallows, dives, and goes off to search for another morsel leaving me only with a view of a broad back of a thing that looks crocodilian from the side, but with a tail fluke that is almost whale-like.

That's a thought that comes later though, because for now I'm too busy drowning, until a hand grabs at me and I'm pulled aboard another lifeboat. Geordie is there, looking like he needs a drink as badly as I do. I look around for the captain but there is no sign of him and most of the others in the boat with us are midshipmen. We bob around in the waves, wondering what the fuck has just happened.

And we're like that for the rest of the longest night of my life, a night spent thinking every breath might be my last, waiting for a beastie to once again cast its scarred eye on me.

Morning brings rescue; eighteen of us in two boats, the only survivors. Once I'm dry and warm and have a smoke and a coffee I tell my story to the brass, then to psychologists, to more brass and eventually to anyone who will listen. Geordie backs me up as far as he can, but he didn't see the creature; only I had that privilege.

My story that a big beastie did it and ran away is not going down well.

Finally they cut me loose; dishonorable discharge or resignation. I chose resignation; it isn't as if there is much of a pension to lose.

After that things get blurry for a time, while I search for the secrets that can only be found at the bottom of whisky bottles.

I search for quite a while.

"Come on, boss," O'Shea says as the world filled in around me again. "Sea serpents? You're taking the piss. This is some twenty-thousand leagues under the sea bollocks you give to the new guy to see how gullible he is, right?"

Geordie replied where I wouldn't, his voice low and soft.

"Look at the man, Roddy," he said. "Does he look like somebody that's taking the piss?"

O'Shea looked at me and I looked back at him. I saw the same disbelief I'd seen from brass and psychologists back then.

"Show him, lad," Geordie said. "He won't believe you otherwise. You ken that We've been through this afore."

"You show him," I replied. "I'm comfortable here."

I stayed in my seat; I hadn't had enough to drink yet and was working hard on improving that situation while Geordie showed O'Shea the files on our recent missions. He pointed at pictures of dead beasts laid out on the deck of what was unmistakable as *The Havenhome.*

"Here's your sea serpents, Roddy. Or as wee Moira calls them, Plesiosaur, Ichthyosaur, Basilosaurus…all beasties thought extinct… all beasties we've caught. It's who we are. It's what we do."

There was more than that but I tuned it out; I'd seen them already. Yes, they were beasties, but they weren't the one I wanted to see dead. The one with the scarred eye was what I was after, and my heart wouldn't rest until either I had it or the booze got me first.

Right now, that race was going the wrong way for me.

Geordie and I finished O'Shea's *initiation* in a time-honored manner; we all got roaring drunk. I remember a disgusted Moira coming in at one point to ask us to stop singing but apart from that much of the night is, mercifully, blank.

I woke, sometime the next morning, to unwelcome sun streaming into my cabin, and Moira shouting at me to get my arse in gear.

"She's back," she said. "And she's pissed off."

-4-

"How do you know it's a she?" Geordie asked Moira. We were all up on the bridge looking at a monitor that suggested that something was definitely watching us as we watched it.

"Because only a woman with the patience of a saint could have put up with your bullshit last night without clocking you one. Now shut the fuck up; some of us are trying to work here."

The instruments showed there was definitely something in the sunken caldera with us. There was no repeat of the howling wails we'd heard the day before but whatever it was, it was a big bugger, and it was circling us in ever decreasing circles. My blood ran cold, remembering again the night in the rain in the North Atlantic.

"Maybe she just wants another tickle," Geordie said, trying for levity.

Moira wasn't having any of it.

"Aye? Well she can get in the queue wi' everybody else."

She turned to me.

"What do you want to do, boss? Sit and wait for it, or go after it?"

Both approaches had worked for us in different circumstances on different hunts, but to tell the truth, neither of them particularly appealed to me that morning; I'd have been happier going back to my bunk with a fresh bottle. But they were all looking to me for a decision; it didn't matter which one I made as long as I made one, so I mentally tossed a coin.

"Let's no' get our knickers in a fankle just yet," I said. "It's a beastie with a plan, that's clear. We'll give it some time to show us if it's got any moves."

"And if it fancies something more than a tickle?" O'Shea said.

Geordie replied for me.

"Oh, we've got plenty of toys to get her excited if that's the kind of mood she's in."

The inward circling stopped when she got within a hundred yards of us. We could tell by the instruments that she was hanging, twenty feet under, parallel with us off the port side. Moira estimated her at forty feet long, and bulky with it. At a third of our length, she was going to give us serious problems if she decided to get rowdy.

"Are we sure it's not just a fucking curious whale?" O'Shea said.

"She's too fast," Moira answered, never taking her eyes off the console. "Unless she's a forty-foot Orca, and that's not something I'd want to tangle with."

"She's no' a whale," Geordie said softly. "Trust us on that."

"Then what the fuck is it?"

""That's what we're trying to find out, if you'd just shut the fuck up for five minutes," Moira said.

I knew her well enough to see that she was even more tetchy than usual; there were too many people in what she considered her personal space. I decided it was time to at least play at being captain.

"O'Shea, get below and make sure there's nothing that's going to fly about if we take another hit. Geordie, you go and check on our toys, make sure they're at hand if we need them sharpish. And tell Ruru to keep an eye open; if she comes up, even for a second, I want him to try and put a balloon on her, two if he gets time."

I got mock salutes from both of them, and I smiled to see that O'Shea's hangover appeared to be at least the match of mine. Then it was time for business.

I opened the hatch to the dumb waiter and shouted down to the scullery.

"Stevie, any chance of a pot of coffee up here?"

Her voice came up muffled from below.

"Sure thing, boss. Five minutes."

I turned back to Moira. She still hadn't taken her eyes off the console.

"Is she doing anything?" I asked.

"Aye. She's watching us, we're watching her, and it looks like every other bit of life in this stretch of water has buggered off to leave us to it."

"Well, we already know she's got a taste for posh yachts. I wonder how she feels about us?"

Moira looked pensive.

"I've got a feeling we're going to find out. We've got ourselves a stand-off here, boss. Who's going to blink first?"

"Not me," I said. "I haven't had a fag yet."

I went out on the wee upper deck around the bridge for a pre-coffee smoke. Ruru was already at the harpoon, gaze fixed on the point off our port side where we knew the thing was lurking. Our two youngest crewmen, deckhands Bailey and Kaminski, were laying out ropes attached to flat material on the foredeck. These things had proved their worth several times for us; a combination of Ruru's aim and, when filled from compressed air on the harpoon's impact, giant balloons that impeded the dives of even the biggest beasties. I knew all we needed was a couple of seconds; Ruru's eye and reflexes would do the rest.

The beastie wasn't ready for games just yet.

A pot of coffee arrived with a clatter up the dumb waiter and Moira brought two mugs out and joined me, taking a smoke when offered. We both stared out to the port side.

"She's a stubborn one," I said.

"Aye. Nearly as bad as you, boss" Moira replied. "How many days did you stare out yon thing in the Bahamas?"

"The beastie wi' all the tentacles? Three, I think. It only had one eye though, so it was at a disadvantage from the start."

That got a laugh, her first of the day before she went serious on me again.

"You know why I called it 'she', don't you, boss?"

I nodded.

"So that I don't think it's him, the big scarry-eyed bugger."

"That's right. And it's not him, is it?"

"Nope, you're right on that, lass. And you know why I ken it's not him?" I was thinking of a jaw big enough to open and take in a full lifeboat as I continued. "Because she's not fucking big enough."

Moira went straight to the monitor when we returned to the bridge.

"Still there," she said. "And still plenty big enough for me."

Geordie arrived at that point. He must have heard her, and he'd just been given an opening for a filthy double-entendre, but either he was slipping or she'd given him a scare earlier because he kept his mouth shut and when he did speak it was to address me.

"The wee toys are all lined up, boss," he said. "Ready to go when we are."

I waved my hand out to the port side.

"It's ladies first today," I said. "We're waiting for her majesty."

"Same as it ever was," Geordie muttered and when I looked up he was staring at Moira's back where she worked at the console.

Her majesty kept us waiting. She hung in the water off our port side while the sun rose almost overhead. The dumb waiter rattled and a plate of ham and cheese rolls arrived for lunch; Stevie always knew the moods of my stomach without needing to be asked.

O'Shea turned up at the bridge door as I was having another coffee to wash the bread down.

"Are we just going to sit here all day?" he asked.

"Why? You got something better to be doing?"

"Well, there was this lass in Hong Kong…"

"Stow it, lad. Not interested." Once again I waved a hand out to the port side. "If I was hungry, then so will she be…sometime."

"That depends on how many rich fuckers' yachts she's had, surely?"

"Aye…and don't call me Shirley."

That didn't even get me a smile; I'm getting old enough that my cultural references are also old enough to have passed into history. As Geordie would say, same as it ever was. I was about to remark on the fact when her majesty finally decided to make her move.

"She's diving," Moira shouted.

"How deep is it here?" I asked.

"Only a hundred feet or so."

"Then she's not going far… at least not downwards. Brace yourself…this might get rough."

"What do you mean, rough?" O'Shea said. I was looking past him out the door at the time and saw what he didn't; the beast came up right beside us like a humpback breaching, sloughing water across the deck. If she'd come back down ten feet closer she'd have landed on top of us but as it was the splash sent a wall of water all across the foredeck. *The Havenhome* bucked underfoot. Stevie swore loudly down in the kitchen as something smashed, O'Shea took a tumble that might have caved his head in on the side of the door if I hadn't caught him and, out on the deck, Ruru stood tall and unperturbed on the harpoon. I didn't see the shot fired; that had happened before the beastie did its belly flop. But I did see the rope snake quickly away across the deck. A second later the balloon was dragged over, already starting to inflate.

You've all seen the movie, right? The shark drags the barrel down into the depths and isn't seen again for hours? This wasn't that movie. The balloon, still expanding, bobbed up seconds later twenty yards off our port bow. Ruru was working full tilt to get the harpoon reloaded but wasn't given time for another shot.

Almost as soon as the balloon surfaced a huge tail fluke rose above it and with two beats of the tail tore the material into pieces. It deflated immediately. There was just enough air left in it for us to retrieve it. We dragged what was left of it aboard and found Ruru's harpoon still attached to the line. There was a sliver, no more than the size of my little finger, of flesh attached to it.

We'd given it a pinprick, little more.

End of round one.

The beastie was already ahead on points.

-5-

Moira insisted on having a closer look at the bit of flesh although I was skeptical that we'd find anything we didn't already know.

She looked up from the microscope in the wee cupboard that passes for our lab after a few minutes of peering.

"It's definitely reptilian."

"No shit, Sherlock. Anything else?"

"What else would there be?" she said. Curiosity satisfied, we headed back upstairs. We'd left Geordie at the helm but he was only too happy to relinquish the post back to Moira.

"No sign of her, boss. Maybe she's feert."

"She didnae look feert ten minutes ago," I replied. "Eyes open, folks. She's still watching us, I can feel it in my bones."

"That's just auld age, lad," Geordie replied, smiling. "Comes to us all in time."

Moira checked the monitors.

"If she's still around, she's out of range of our gear here. Nowt on the hydrophones either… maybe Geordie's right. Maybe we scared her off."

I shook my head. I knew this game too well to be complacent.

"We're back to the standoff. Just because we can't see or hear her doesn't mean the same from her viewpoint. We assume she's coming back, and we stay alert. Get the coffee going…it could be a long night."

When coffee arrived, I took a mug out to Ruru who still stood at his post at the harpoon, his gaze firmly fixed out to the port side as if willing the beast to return.

"I hit it fair and square, boss," he said. "Right in the middle of its belly. But it must be as tough as old boots…it looks like the harpoon only penetrated a couple of inches."

"You got a good look at her as she came out of the water," I said. "Any idea what she is?"

Ruru shook his head.

"I know what it's not. It's not a whale, and it's not a crocodile. Somewhere in between."

That left a lot of room for speculation, but Ruru wasn't the kind to overreach and commit himself to an opinion without having stacks of evidence to back it up. For now, I would just go on and call it a beastie. Latin names only give monsters legitimacy anyway, and I have no need to intellectually respect the things I hunt.

"Come on, lad, you can do better than that. What's your best guess?"

"Let's just say I've never seen anything that big that wasn't a whale and leave it at that."

For once I was a step ahead of him, even though I'd much rather that wasn't the case.

Geordie called me back to the bridge.

"The AUV's picking up something."

The bot's sensors told us it was at the farthest point of its circle away from us, near the caldera wall to the north. So far, its camera had been showing us only clear water in its path, but now there was something else, a darker shadow. Moira understood first.

"It's her. She's tracking the bot, just a few yards off to the left there. Look."

She used her finger on the monitor to point out what she meant, and once you saw the shadow that moved along in the same direction and at the same speed it was unmistakable. Our wee bot had found itself a new pal.

"Maybe she is more like a whale after all?" Moira said. "We've seen them taking bots into their pods in the past."

"Aye, maybe. Or maybe she's just taking the piss," Geordie replied.

"Aye. You'd ken all about that, Geordie McCallum."

Whatever was going on, or not going on, between them, I wasn't going to let it get in the way of the hunt. I had to give them something else to think about.

"At least we ken where she is," I said. I turned to Geordie and Moira. "Is there any way we can use this to our advantage?"

"Well, we can tell the bot where to go," Moira said. "If she keeps following it, we can get her where we want her."

"That's a big if," Geordie answered. I agreed, but if there was a chance to get ahead of the game I had to take it.

"Where's the shallowest part of the caldera?" I asked. As I knew she would, Moira answered without having to consider it.

"Over near the west wall. There's a shelf there, about forty feet under."

"...and if we can get her there, we can cramp her style, put the fight on our chosen ground. I like it. Get the bot ready, Moira. Take it on a track heading to the west...but softly does it. We don't want to scare the beastie off by doing anything sudden. And Geordie, rally the crew. We need to be ready for any chance that comes along."

A sense of anticipation grew on the bridge over the next five minutes as Moira headed the AUV over to the west and piloted *The Havenhome* to follow a couple of hundred yards in its wake. I kept a close eye on the monitor; the beastie was still tracking alongside the bot and was showing no sign of deviating from the course we were setting it.

Geordie arrived back at the bridge door.

"We've got two depth charges ready to go at the stern; all you have to do is press the button. Ruru's in his usual place, and there's three more of yon balloons laid out. I've got Bailey and Kaminski primed to reload the harpoon sharpish when it's needed, and I'll be out on the deck keeping an eye on things. O'Shea's in the engine room in case of trouble, and Stevie says she's keeping her head doon… you ken what she's like when it comes to the hard bit."

I did know; for all her aptitude with a variety of blades our cook was remarkably squeamish when it came to the kill at the end of a hunt. It was probably for the best that she stayed below for the duration; at least that gave me one less person to worry about.

And my worries increased a notch a minute later when Moira spoke up.

"The bot's reached the shallow water and her majesty is still right with her. It's your call now, boss."

"Have the bot run in a wee circle around the area," I said. "But stay in the shallows."

"What about us?" Moira said from the helm chair.

"We'll hang here, see if she surfaces. If she does, Ruru will have her. Just creep in slowly, not enough to alarm her. If she lets us get close enough, we'll drop a charge and see how she handles a real fright."

My instincts were proven right over the next few minutes; the beastie kept tracking the AUV around in the shallows, and seemed oblivious to the fact that *The Havenhome* was slowly creeping closer to the both of them. Moira had a quiet hand at the helm and I knew we were making little if any engine noise on our approach.

Moira counted down the distance between us.

"A hundred yards, boss. You know that if we drop a charge in this shallow water, we're liable to blow a hole in our own keel?"

"Not if we fuck off out of the way fast enough."

"That's your plan? Throw a banger at her and run away? What age are you, eight?"

"And a half. Come on, Moira. It's worked before."

"That time in the Azores? When you blew off a propeller, we were in dry dock for a month, you damn near went bankrupt and we lived on bananas for a fortnight? That time it worked?"

Geordie laughed, then went quiet when I gave him one of my looks.

"We killed the critter, didn't we?"

"Ninety yards," she said, and that was to be the end of that as she used her back to show me her disapproval. To be fair, it was a very disapproving back.

"Eighty yards."

"How's her majesty?"

"Still dancing with the AUV. Seventy-five yards."

I turned to Geordie.

"What's your gut saying? Think she'll let us get on top of her?"

He was looking at Moira when he spoke, and smiling.

"Depends on her mood. You can never tell with women."

Moira flicked him a V with her left hand without looking round.

"Seventy yards. If you're going to do anything apart from go right at her, now would be the time."

"Come round to port and let the back end drift, see how close we can get the stern to her."

"We're going to be making a fuck of a mess of the AUV, boss," Geordie said.

"I'll buy O'Shea a new one; we're getting paid enough."

"Sixty yards and coming about. I think she's taking an interest, boss. She's coming closer. Forty yards."

"Drop the charge and leg it," I shouted.

Moira didn't waste time questioning me. She pushed the button and I heard a rumble from the back end as the charge was freed. Then the engines kicked in full throttle and we began to move away.

"We're much too close," Moira shouted. "Brace for impact."

I heard a muffled "Oh, fuck," from the galley down below then the whole back end of the boat lifted and smacked back down hard. I was already out of my seat, heading for the foredeck, and got there just in time to see the beast rise up at our stern, mouth agape as if she had identified the source of the attack on it and was ready to have a piece of it. I caught a flicker of movement in my peripheral vision, turned and saw Ruru standing up straight at the harpoon.

The beast was every bit as huge as I'd imagined her to be, but the charge had done a job on her; she had a hole the size of a door in her left flank and she moved sluggishly, as if concussed. Ruru didn't need a second invitation and he'd learned his lesson well on our first encounter. I heard the hiss of the harpoon as it flew straight and true across the deck to embed itself dead center in the thing's cold left eye. She was dead before the balloon started to inflate. Ruru put a second harpoon into the other eye for good measure. The beast started to sink. The balloons fully inflated with a pop. I was able to walk over to the stern, look down and see the massive body floating some twenty feet below us, trailing a river of blood in our wake.

I turned to find Moira and Geordie at my back and let out a yell of triumph.

"I told you it would work. That's how the professionals get the job done."

- 6 -

"You fucked up my bot, boss," O'Shea said ten minutes later. Ruru, Bailey and Kaminski were on the winches trying to get the beast's head out of the water so we could take some photographs. The engineer had hauled in the AUV, what was left of it. It might still run but it likely wasn't going to be of much use as various different circuit boards were fried, the camera had smashed and only one of the twin propellers was still operable.

"As I told Geordie, I'm good for another one."

"I'll hold you to that, boss," he said with a smile. "But first, I've got questions."

"I'm sure you do, lad. Ask away, I'll answer those I can and give you my best guess at those I can't."

"First, and the biggest one…where the fuck did that thing come from?"

I laughed.

"Ah, the easy one first. Ask Stevie, if she'll talk to you. She's got theories by the dozen; a hollow earth, a rift in space-time, atomic mutations, genetic scientists and wee green men are all candidates in the big pot of theories. But you ken that; I ken you've seen the same films I have."

"Aye. And if a big angry gorilla ever turns up I'm outta here fast."

"You and me both, lad. But to answer your question… does it matter? I mean, they're here, obviously. We just killed one and I personally don't give a fuck where she came from as long as she's dead."

That got me another of his smiles.

"Next question then… what happens now?"

"Now we get paid. And I'm betting yon yacht club has some fancy toys for sale. I think we'll go and see how the other half live. And there'll be some posh women for you to eye up, so double bonus."

"I'll hold you to that too."

I left him with the remains of the bot and headed for my cabin for, first, a wee celebratory dram, and second, to make my first, and only, report to the money man.

By the time I got my laptop up and running Moira and Geordie already had some photies loaded up on our server. Moira had even, tentatively, made an identification, *Shonisaurus*, some kind of bloody big *Ichthyosaur*. As I've said, I didn't care what it was called; what it meant to me was cash, and lots of it.

Getting that cash out of Franks proved to be as hard as expected. The webcam feed showed him sitting, prim and proper behind the big desk. If he was at all impressed, he wasn't showing it.

"How do I know that's what's been taking out our members' yachts?" was his first question on seeing the photographs.

"You think there's two of these fuckers in the same waters at the same time? How about we check its stomach contents? I'm betting we can come up with some of the Russian billionaire's tart if we dig about. We could send the bits back to him."

My attempt at humor was totally lost on him; he took me seriously.

"There will be no need for that, I'm sure. It's just that I will be shelling out a lot of money for this job; I need to know it's done."

"The thing's as dead as a very dead thing," I replied. "It's done. The only question now is how you want it to be handled."

"Handled?"

"I mean, what do you want done with it? You paid for it, it's yours. We can deliver what's left of the body, or just the head if you'd like; it would make a fine trophy, mounted in your hotel, although you might need a bigger ballroom to exhibit it properly."

Again, any attempt at humor went way over his head.

"Oh, our members wouldn't like that at all. No. I've seen the pictures, that's all I need. Dispose of it as you see fit."

"And the money?"

He looked pained to speak of it.

"I'll have it wired to your account forthwith."

"It was a pleasure doing business with you," I said.

"I wish I could say the same," he replied, and hung up on me before I could get there first.

"So what do we do with it?" O'Shea asked.

An impromptu party had started up in the galley; Stevie had got a few cases of beer out and was busy prepping pizza, Geordie and O'Shea were already on the whisky and Bailey and Kaminski were making inroads into the aforesaid beer. Stevie had even sent a couple of beers up the hatch for Moira at the helm. The only member of the crew not in a party mood appeared to be Ruru; he was still up on deck, just sitting staring at the beast where we had it hoisted, head out of the water, tail trailing behind us.

"Communing with his prey," Stevie had said. "Best to leave him to it."

Moira called down asking for direction.

"Drop anchor and come and join the party," I shouted back. "We're in no hurry to get anywhere."

As to the question as to what to do with the dead thing, that was something that had been on my mind.

"We could sell it," O'Shea said. "Surely some scientist..."

"...would want to know why we found one of the rarest beasties on the planet, something supposed to be extinct for over a hundred million years, and our first reaction was to blow the shite out of it?" I answered.

"But still, there must be value in it?"

"Only if we tell somebody what we did. And the fly wee bugger Franks made me sign a non-disclosure agreement. If we break it, we get sued, and he's the type that would enjoy it, believe you me."

"I know a man who knows a man in Hong Kong who would take it off our hands, no questions asked," O'Shea replied.

"I probably ken the same man," I answered. "And the answer's still no. Like I said, Franks is a fly wee bugger. He'll have all his bases covered watching for us to fuck up. I ken the type."

"So just cut it adrift?"

I shrugged. I was more interested in the whisky Geordie was pouring for me.

"We could eat it," Stevie said, and got a laugh all round. "No, seriously. It looks almost like a big croc. I've had alligator steaks and they're delicious. I…"

O'Shea was still laughing.

"Get that knife you were ready to use on me and go cut a chunk out of it. We'll fry it up and have a taste, see if you're right. I dare you."

Stevie, never one to back down on a dare, took him at his word and went up on deck with her biggest knife. I was onto my second whisky and starting to feel mellow by the time she returned. I knew immediately from her face that something was up, and it wasn't likely to be anything good.

"There's something you all need to see," she said, and wouldn't be drawn any further until we all got on deck.

Ruru was at the stern, under the body of the beast near the tail end. There was a wide gaping gash in the body above him, still dripping fluid. Ruru seemed to be using one of the fire axes to chop at something that squirmed on the deck below him. I had to move close to see. Whatever it was, it stank and I had to cover my mouth to get closer still.

Ruru stood over the dead carcasses of what looked to be a score, maybe more, of embryonic beasts, each no more than the length of my arm. He stood above the last one. It squirmed, mewled in a wail pitifully reminiscent of the one we'd heard on the hydrophone, then the axe came down and the deck area fell silent.

"For fuck's sake, Stevie," O'Shea said. "I asked for a steak, not sushi."

We filtered back to the galley leaving Ruru behind; he insisted he'd be the one to clear up the mess. All thought of eating was gone for the time being, but drinking began in earnest.

"That man in Hong Kong would have paid a fortune for those babbies," O'Shea said. "And your man at the yacht club need have been none the wiser."

I nodded; I'd already thought of that.

"You're missing the point," I replied.

"Which is?"

"The wee man in the yacht club is going to be very pissed off to find out that we killed mammy beastie."

"Mammy or not, it's still dead."

"You're still missing the point. Where there's a mammy and babbies, there's a daddy. Whoever he is, he's still out there somewhere. And when he does show up, the wee fucker in the yacht club's going to want his money back."

- 7 -

"So what's the plan, boss?"

Moira, as ever, was trying to be the voice of reason. All I wanted to do was get pished and forget about everything else till morning, but she wasn't going to let me have any of that.

"The way I see it we don't have much choice; if there's another wan o' these buggers about here, we're going to have to find it and kill it, before word gets back to the fucker in the yacht club. It's the only way we'll get paid."

"So, no rich totty for me then?" O'Shea said.

"At least not in the immediate future," I replied.

"And how do we find this other beastie?" Geordie asked. "We ken it's not in the area, otherwise we'd have picked it up on the monitors by now."

"Well, we found this one well enough by tracking where it had fed. Let's assume it was the other one that got tangled with the Russian's yacht… if we do that, at least we've got somewhere to start."

"Aye," Geordie said. "A fifty-fifty chance you're wrong."

"And a fifty-fifty chance I'm right."

I had Moira get back to the helm and chart a course to the Russian's position where the accident happened. It was going to take several hours to get there, hours I'd rather spend with the whisky, but I put a stop to the party… the drinking part of it anyway, and took some pizza out for Ruru, who was once again sitting on the deck contemplating the corpse of the beastie.

"We shouldn't have killed it," were his first words to me, and the first time I'd ever known him to rue the results of a successful hunt.

"You're not going soft on me, are you? I didnae think it was in your nature."

"Not so much in my nature as in my bones," he replied. "The ancestors say it's bad luck for a year to kill anything that's pregnant."

"Awa' and don't talk pish, man," I replied. "We're baith auld enough to ken the difference between what's real and what's auld fisherwives' stories."

"And I'm old enough to know that old men make the greatest fools when they get set in their ways. We shouldn't have done it. That's all I'll say on the matter. Can we dump it?"

"Fine by me," I replied. "Dragging it about like this will only get us attention we don't want. We've got the photos, we've been paid, let it go. Besides, we've got bigger fish to fry."

I didn't push it. I told him about going after the other one and he merely nodded.

"I'll be ready," he said, and when I left him he was already using the winches to lower the carcass into the water.

I ordered the rest of the crew to get their heads down while they still could then went to join Moira on the bridge. Night was falling and a wash of starlight was beginning to cover the sky.

"You should practice what you preach and get your head down too, boss," Moira said. "I've got this."

"Never you mind that," I replied. I lit up a smoke and waved out at the view. "Third star on the left and straight on till morning. You know the drill."

This was my favorite part, just us, the night and the stars, Moira at the helm, me in the captain's seat, a mug of coffee, a smoke and a wee drop of the good stuff. It's as close to contentment as I get, and I wouldn't have it any other way. I even managed to forget about the mess we'd seen on deck a few hours earlier; it only came back to mind near midnight as we rounded a point and headed into the bay where the Russian had had his encounter.

We were not the only boat in the area; it looked like this was party country for the rich and infamous. Three yachts, each larger and more gaudy than the other, were anchored up offshore and there was a large bonfire on the beach with scores of people milling around it. The thump of a dance beat carried across the water.

"What now, boss?" Moira said.

"Drop anchor, lay low and try to look inconspicuous," I replied. "Then we switch all the toys on and wait. You can go and get your head down if you like; I'll keep the watch."

"No, you're okay, boss. Besides, leaving you alone with that bottle isn't the best idea in the world."

"Touché, Madame Pussycat," I said in my best mouse impression, and I got that look again. As I said, my cultural reference points are getting too old. I let it go over her head as she dropped anchor and cut the engines. We were moored almost a mile offshore, at the mouth of a wide crescent bay. It rose to a mountainous wooded peak behind the fire on the shore but either end of the crescent was bare rock blasted by salt spray and sun. Nothing moved out here, not even us and we bobbed, almost pleasantly, in a small swell.

The night passed slowly. For once I was able to keep the drinking down to a slow sip, the dance beat continued its monotonous but compelling beat from the shore and Stevie kept a flow of coffee coming up from the galley. I was feeling pretty mellow and on the verge of nodding off to sleep when Moira spoke softly from the helm.

"Heads up, boss. I think we've got company."

I heard the faint bleep from the radar monitor that confirmed her suspicion.

"How big?" I asked.

"Big enough to be our pal," she replied. "And moving fast, coming into the bay. Shall I get everybody up?"

"Not yet. Not until we're sure; it feels too neat for it to be our boy just when we get here."

"Neat's good. I like neat."

"I don't," I replied. "Neat's a three bedroom house, wife and kids and an SUV in the garage."

"What's wrong with that, boss?"

I waved a hand at the sea and the night and the stars.

"Everything," I said, and smiled to show her I didn't mean it. I knew she didn't believe me, and she knew I knew so all round, it was already pretty neat and sewn up.

The radar beeped again.

"Still coming," Moira said. "Big and fast, just like her Majesty. Bigger by the looks of it."

"Bugger," I said. "Okay. Get everybody up. And try the radio, see if you can hail any of yon yachts."

"And what would I tell them, boss? A sea monster is coming? They'll think I've been on the waccy-baccy."

"Let them think it; they need to be warned. Whether they listen or not is up to them."

The next few minutes had the boat a hive of activity as the rest of the crew were roused blearily from their bunks. When I got up and went out on the foredeck Ruru was already at the harpoon and Bailey and Kaminski were laying out fresh balloons; I knew they were the last two from the stockroom; I hoped I wouldn't have to be ordering more any time soon. Geordie and O'Shea were rolling another depth charge to the stern.

"How about the AUV?" I asked. "Is there any use of getting her in the water?"

"She'll be swimming blind and lopsided, but I think the hydrophone's still in working order if you need it?"

"I think we need it," I said, but we weren't given time to deploy it. Moira shouted from the bridge.

"It's here. Right below us."

I went to the rail and looked down, but all I saw was black water, although I felt the boat rise and fall on a swell that didn't feel like a normal wave.

"Which way?" I shouted.

"Into the bay, heading right for those yachts."

I ran back into the bridge.

"Did you warn them?"

"I tried. One didn't answer, one told me to 'take a chill pill' and the third told me to fuck off, so off I fucked."

"Bugger."

"My sentiments exactly."

"Get that anchor up," I said. "We might need to move quickly."

My worry was that any move we had to make was going to be to rescue survivors. I didn't mention it to Moira; I didn't have to; I saw the same fear in her eyes.

I went back onto deck and tried to peer into the night, tried to will myself to see the beast, but there was only the dark sea and the sky, and when the attack came on the yachts it was almost as much a surprise to me as it must have been to them.

The first sign was a booming thud, loud above the dance beat from shore. All the lights went out on the smaller of the three yachts, making it just a slightly darker patch of shadow on the water, and then, a couple of seconds later, I couldn't see it at all. I heard the screams well enough though, the panic and terror echoing around the bay.

The larger of the two remaining yachts began to move towards the location of the screams.

"Moira, get us moving. They're going to need our help."

Geordie came to my side and he too peered into the darkness.

"Did it take out a yacht?"

"Looks that way," I said, then could only watch in horror as the lights on the yacht that had been heading towards the screams tipped up, the horizontal becoming almost vertical before falling back towards the sea. Then they too went out, this time with a loud, explosive bang. Fire followed, flames running the length of the yacht's deck, and there were more screams, both from on the water and from the shore, where the party had come to an abrupt end.

The boat moved under us; Moira had got the anchor up and was turning our prow towards the stricken yachts. I knew in my heart we were already far too late.

I had Geordie turn on the big flood light at the prow as we headed at speed towards the carnage; that was when we got our only glimpse of the perpetrator. It was heading back out of the bay, swimming almost at the surface and raising a bow wave. Its head came up on our starboard side, meaning that Ruru couldn't get a shot at it. I had time to get a good look at it; it was at least eighty feet long if it was an inch, a lot of it was teeth and jaw and the bastard looked like it was smiling at us.

It wasn't the scar-eyed face of my nightmares, but I knew right there and then that I wouldn't get any rest until I'd hunted this fucker down.

- 8 -

We did what we could to help out and air-sea rescue choppers were on scene less than an hour after Moira sent out a Mayday, but the count came to twenty dead, as many again injured, two multi-million pound yachts reduced to flotsam and a bloody mess that was going to be worldwide news in a matter of hours.

The expected video call came in just as the sun was coming up and the last of the wounded were being lifted out. I wasn't in any mood to be polite.

"What the fuck do you want?" was my opening gambit, and it kind of went downhill fast from there.

"There has been another attack," he said. He was back in the big chair again, and I really wanted to punch that smug little grin right through the monitor.

"No shit, Sherlock. Want to come and help us scoop the bits out of the water?"

"No, what I want is for you to do your job," he replied. The grin was still there. It reminded me of the thing that had passed us in the water in the night.

"My job's done," I said. "Contract said kill the beastie, I killed it, I got paid. Thanks and goodbye."

"You didn't actually read the contract, did you?" he answered, and the grin was now so smug I knew I was beaten as he continued. "It clearly mentions that the contract will not be fulfilled until the threat is nullified. Not the beastie… the threat. I'd say last night's losses could be considered a threat, wouldn't you? As for payment. That has, of course, been withheld until you hold up your end of the deal."

"I'll tell you what I'd like to hold up," I said, but I was talking to empty air. The wee bastard had hung up on me again.

I didn't tell the others about the money situation; they get paid whether I do or not so it wasn't worth giving them something else to worry about. For the moment at least, we all had our hands full with helping the authorities with the wounded, trying to keep our story straight as to why we were in the area, and keeping our mouths firmly shut against any talk of sea monsters.

The media weren't holding anything back; they only had photos of wreckage and bodybags to show, but plenty of the survivors were more than willing to talk. My favorite quote came from an Aussie, one of the deckhands from the larger yacht.

"I'm telling you, it was fucking Godzilla."

Speculation was rife… and we were the subject of much of it. I decided discretion was the better part of valor and, after checking with the authorities it was okay, ordered Moira to take us out of the bay.

"What heading, boss?"

"I don't really give a fuck right now. Just get us out of here. I need some quiet to think in."

We crept off as unobtrusively as a hundred and twenty footer can manage. One of the news choppers followed us out of the bay then lost interest and returned to the still growing media circus on the shore by the smoldering remains of last night's bonfire. I waited for an hour to make sure nobody else was paying us any interest, then told Moira to head back to the caldera where we'd found the first one.

"A hunch, boss?"

"Aye, but little more than that. I figured her Majesty had to get pregnant somewhere, and the place we found her is as good a spot to start as any. Just keep your eyes on the monitors. If the big lad is like his wife, he might fancy a dance."

The big lad proved to be shy; there was no sign of him on our return journey. Moira was managing to monitor both our equipment and at least half a dozen news channels at the same time, all while piloting the boat. Me, I was having enough trouble just getting a smoke lit. I went out on deck into a hot morning and found Ruru cleaning and oiling the harpoon gun.

"This one's going to be bad, boss," he said as he took an offered cigarette from me. "I feel it in my bones."

"Your ancestors giving you a hard time again?"

"Ever since last night. And they're getting louder."

"Well tell them to pipe down; I'm off for a nap. If anybody needs anything, Moira's in charge."

"Same as it ever was," Ruru replied, in a remarkably accurate imitation of wee Geordie. I was still smiling as I went back to the bridge, but any good humor was to prove to be short lived, and my nap was postponed indefinitely.

One of the reporters on the beach in the bay was obviously good at his job. Moira was running his report, most of it about us. He'd already tracked down several of our previous jobs, both wins and failures, emphasizing the latter, and was currently speculating who our employer might be. The wee smug bastard back at the yacht club wasn't going to like that one bit, but I couldn't even take pleasure in that thought. Any chance we had of anonymity on this one was well and truly blown. All I could hope for was that they wouldn't know to look for us in the caldera, for if they came hunting in their usual pack for us our chances of finding, let alone killing, the big lad were slim to none.

I fretted over that all the way back to the caldera. Even Stevie's coffee failed to revive my mood and by mid-afternoon I was itching to head for my cabin and make some inroads in the whisky bottle. I might even have done so if Moira hadn't piped up from the helm just as the caldera came into sight on the horizon.

"Getting a ping on the radar, boss. Port side, about a hundred yards. That's twice now. I think we're being checked out."

"Maybe he fancies that dance after all," I said. "Don't make any sudden moves; with any luck he'll follow us all the way in, and we'll see if he'll fall for the same trap as his missus."

Any hope I had of us being left alone to get on with hunting the beastie down was dashed as soon as we entered the caldera. There was a news chopper there already, one of those amphibious jobs with fitted floats, and it had touched down slap bang in the middle of the area. To make matters worse, they were determined to be chatty. I let Moira fend them off and went back out on deck to see if I could shift what was threatening to become a thumper of a headache. Geordie was outside having a smoke with Ruru and I went to join them.

"It's nice to be popular, eh, boss?" Geordie said, waving a hand towards the chopper. "Have they offered you any moolah for our story yet?"

"If you're taking the piss, I'm warning you, I'm not in the mood," I replied.

"What's not to like?" Geordie replied. "The press are having a field day at our expense, and I'm betting yon wee mannie at the yacht club is a bundle of joy too. Anything I can do for you?"

"I appreciate the offer. Just keep an eye on the reporters. Make sure they stay over there. If any of them tries to come aboard, you have my permission to kick their arses."

During this exchange, Ruru had kept his eyes fixed on a point several hundred yards behind us on the starboard side, just inside the entrance to the caldera.

"Something?" I asked.

He waved his hand in a see-saw manner.

"Fifty-fifty at the moment. But I think he's following us."

"Moira's wee toys agree with you. Eyes open, lads. This could go down fast if it comes for us."

"What about the reporters?" Geordie asked. "Should we warn them there might be a beastie in the area?"

"Nah, fuck 'em. They'd just make a report about it. Let them take their chances."

I headed for the stern and found O'Shea, Bailey and Kaminski working on the AUV. It certainly looked much improved from when we'd brought it out of the water, but even my untrained eye could see that it was pretty badly fucked up.

"What's not working?" I asked.

"Better just to say what is," O'Shea replied. "We've got the hydrophone, and I've jury-rigged a camera so we'll get some pictures, but it's not live-cam, just a shot every ten seconds or so. She'll send the photos back to us, but we won't be able to tell her where to go; navigation is irreparable. She'll go in a big circle when we put her in the water, and keep doing that until something gets in her way."

I patted him on the shoulder.

"Nice work anyway," I said. "It can't have been easy getting even that much out of her."

"That's why you pay me the big bucks, boss," he replied with a grin.

Any reply I might have given was aborted by a loud splash off our starboard side. I turned in time to see Ruru stand up at the harpoon, but he wasn't taking aim and by the time I hurried over to his position there was nothing to see but ripples on the water. I saw Geordie's face well enough though, and the astonishment showing large.

"We're going to need bigger charges, boss," he said. "He just slapped his fluke at us and if that's any indication of his overall size, he's fucking enormous."

"And maybe even bigger than that," Ruru said with a thin smile. The harpoonist wasn't looking behind us now; his gaze was directed almost directly ahead. I saw why when something broke the surface of the water halfway between us and the chopper. It moved like an Orca, swift and purposeful… and much bigger.

"Fuck. Moira!" I shouted. "Tell those fucking reporters to get in the air. Right fucking now."

The chopper pilot had already got the message; I guessed he'd got a glimpse of what was coming for him. The next few seconds seemed to happen in slow motion. The chopper rotors got up to speed quickly and it began to lift, front end first, off the surface. The beastie surfaced again. We were directly in line behind it and saw the tail fin sweep in a rise and fall that drove it forward at speed. I was doing mental calculations; it was going to be a close thing. It looked like the chopper pilot knew it too, for he hit his throttle before he was properly in the air and the chopper took a violent lurch. It did, however, give him an extra second of breathing space as the beast had to make a course correction. It was enough time for the machine to gain lift, ten, fifteen, twenty feet up and climbing fast now.

Not fast enough.

The beast dived some thirty yards from the chopper's position then, seconds later, came up, head first, directly under it. When it opened its jaws the span of its gape was wide enough to take the whole body of the machine inside with room to spare and, just as it reached the highest point of its leap, the mouth snapped shut. Two rotor blades flew far and wide but it took the rest down with it as it hit the water with an enormous splash. It submerged immediately, and nothing of the chopper came back up, although we spent the best part of half an hour looking.

- 9 -

"We really need to tell somebody, boss," Moira said once I decided to call off the search for survivors.

"No, we really don't," I replied. "Not if we ever want to get this job one. Telling somebody means authorities, and more reporters. You think they were bad before? One of their own has gone now; they'll be like a terrier going after a rabbit. They'll never let up. No. We just got here. We don't know what happened to them. We never saw them. If anybody turns up to ask, that's the story and we stick to it."

"I'm not sure I can do that," Moira said.

"And I'm not sure I give a fuck. We either get this job done, or we all go out to pasture. It's as simple as that. And I'm not taking questions."

That got me a view of her disapproving back again, and very impressive it was too. After a minute or so I'd had enough of that so I went back out on deck. Ruru was still at the harpoon station.

"Any sign of him?"

"Nope. I'm guessing a whole chopper takes a bit of digesting," he replied deadpan.

"Did he follow us from yon bay last night or did we follow him?"

He gave me the see-saw hand wave again.

"A bit of both I think, boss. He has his instincts, and you have yours."

"Did your ancestors tell you to say that," I said, laughing.

I only got a smile in reply but it was enough to improve my mood slightly as I headed astern where O'Shea had just stood up away from the AUV.

"She's as ready as she's ever going to be," he said. "Shall I get her in the water?"

"Please, do. If we get very lucky the big bugger will want to dance, and we can trap him the same way as we did the pregnant one."

"Given the way he took the chopper down, I don't think this one's much of a dancer."

"That's okay. Neither am I. But I ken how to lead."

"Speaking of which," he said, leaning in close and lowering his voice. "You need to have a wee word with Stevie. She's upset."

"Of course she's fucking upset. If you kept yer hands to yerself she'd have a whole lot less to be upset about."

"No, it's not that," he answered. "I caught her crying in the galley earlier. She wouldn't say what about, but she was talking about handing in her notice as soon as we reach a port."

"Oh for fuck's sake, spare me from emotional women," I muttered.

"Send them my way if you like," O'Shea answered, but by then I was already heading for the galley.

As I mentioned earlier, Stevie and I have a history, but I was only a page in hers, one of many ships that had passed her in the night. Stevie cultivated man trouble like a professional and I was ready for another tale of woe and love found and lost again, a story I'd heard over many a bottle of whisky in the depths of calm nights at sea. But if that was the problem this time, she wasn't ready to talk about it, at least not to me. A frown turned quickly to anger as soon as she turned and saw me in the galley entrance.

"Fuck off. I'm not talking to you."

"What did I do this time?"

"It's what you didn't do," she said, and showed me a back every bit as disapproving as Moira's had been earlier. Seems it was my day for pissing off the womenfolk. As Geordie would say, same as it ever was.

"Give me a clue here, lass. That could be a long list."

"What part of fuck off aren't you understanding?"

I fucked off, headed up to the bridge and asked Moira if she knew what Stevie's problem was.

Moira told me to fuck off.

I was just about old enough and wise enough to know when I was beat. I left Geordie in charge with orders to rouse me if the beastie made an appearance and headed for my bunk in the hope that a couple of hours sleep would help sort things out. I was woken what seemed like seconds later by a banging on the cabin door.

"Time to get your arse in gear, lad," Geordie shouted. "We've got company."

I was surprised to find that four hours had gone by, and even more surprised to find that the company referred to wasn't more reporters, but the big beast. He'd turned up on Moira's console again, a blip at the edge of the radar, prowling around us like a big cat looking for an opening.

"There's something else, boss," Moira said. "We had a call from local Air-Sea Rescue. They're looking for a lost chopper."

"What did you tell them?"

"That we just got here and didn't see anything," she said. I saw by her eyes she still didn't like it, and it came to me that I already knew why Stevie was so pissed off at me too. I may be slow, but I get there in the end. O'Shea settled the matter for me by arriving with photies of the chopper wreck taken by the AUV; it was lying in a shallow spot, some thirty feet deep. It would also be the perfect place for us to lay an ambush, but when I looked in Moira's eyes, I knew what had to be done.

"Call it in for me, lass, would you? Tell them we've found debris and are ready to provide assistance."

She sent me a smile… a thin one that didn't quite reach her eyes, but it was a start, at least.

"What about the beastie, boss?" Geordie said from the doorway.

"If we can wait a bit, so can he," I replied. "But if he comes after us…or anyone else for that matter… while we're getting that chopper up, then all bets are off and God save us."

O'Shea volunteered to go down and get some chains on the debris. I wasn't keen on letting him take the risk, but there had been no new blips on the radar, and the Air-Sea rescue lads were still en-route. I figured it would be better PR for us to be actually doing something when they arrived, so I let the Irishman get suited up.

"If I end up as that beast's supper, I'll be back to haunt you," he said as he stood in the cage ready to be winched down.

"As long as you know there's a queue," I replied, and turned away; I wasn't ready for any of his witticisms at that moment. The rattle of chains as the winch let him down sounded like the ghosts that haunted my conscience. I went back to my cabin on the way to the bridge and allowed myself a stiffener of two fingers of the good Scotch; I figured I was going to need it.

- 10 -

As it turned out, O'Shea's dive went smooth and by the numbers. He got the chains onto the debris and we slowly winched it up on deck. Everybody but Stevie turned out for a look; there wasn't much to see but a mangled mess that looked like it had been put through a crusher. If there were any bodies in there, they were beyond recognition as anything that might once have been human.

The amphibious rescue chopper arrived minutes later, and I had my heart in my mouth as it came down for a landing, expecting his Majesty to make an entrance at any moment. But maybe the first chopper had given him indigestion, for he didn't turn up for second helpings.

I spent a bad half hour fending questions from the rescue guys. I could tell they didn't quite believe my story, but my crew backed me up and our three wise monkeys act, plus the obvious fact that we couldn't have been responsible for the mangled wreck on our deck, meant that they eventually left us alone and tended to the wreckage.

They had a coastguard vessel sent to us; luckily it was in the general area so only took a couple of hours, but for every minute of it I was on tenterhooks, expecting an attack from below. I was on edge, my crew was on edge, the rescue guys knew something wasn't right, and we had a wrecked chopper and two, maybe three lost men. Everything about the situation stank to high heaven.

But, finally, and after what seemed an age, the coastguard boat turned up, the chopper wreckage was carefully and respectfully winched away and we were allowed to leave the scene, but not before I was ordered to make a full report at my earliest convenience to the authorities in Manilla. I'd already decided my earliest convenience was going to be sometime never, but neglected to tell them that; I don't think they were in the mood.

By the time it was all done, we had got the AUV out of the water and I'd had Moira take us ten miles north to anchor in a, thankfully, empty bay, it was getting round to dusk again, and my crew were as cranky as they ever get.

Stevie still wasn't talking to me, but at least Moira had softened somewhat, at least enough that the atmosphere on the bridge was no longer frigid. There was, however, still something going on between her and Geordie that was causing my First Mate to keep well away. He, O'Shea, Bailey and Kaminski had a pretty raucous, and acrimonious card game going on in the small room that serves as our mess; I could hear the arguments coming up the dumb waiter and they were getting heated enough that I was going to have to get off my arse sooner rather than later.

At least Ruru was being his usual dependable self; he was still standing at the harpoon station, still gazing out over the increasingly darkening water, like a sentry on duty which, I suppose, in a way he was.

As for me, I was still tetchy after our encounter with the authorities, and my mood wasn't helped by the fact that Moira informed me I had three emails waiting for me from Franks at the yacht club. I intended to ignore the wee tosser for as long as possible and vowed that I'd be drunk if I had to speak to him again.

The only good thing about the day so far was that the beastie hadn't attacked us. But that also meant we'd had no chance to make any attempt at catching it, something I intended to rectify as soon as the coastguard and rescue team had decided to stop searching for the reporters' dead bodies. That might take some time though, and I knew that would only lead to ever increasing tensions among my crew. They needed action as much as I did, but I could see little prospect of it in our immediate future.

I'd been sitting quietly contemplating the ruin of the day when Moira spoke up softly from the console.

"We've got company again, boss. He's a curious big bugger, I'll give him that."

I went over to the console and she showed me the blip, tight on the edge of our radar, hanging back on the starboard side, same as before.

"Maybe he is a dancer after all," I said. "Keep an eye on him. I'll go tell Ruru."

I wasn't at all surprised to see that Ruru already had his gaze fixed on a spot off the starboard side.

"About a hundred yards back, and not coming any closer, boss," he said. "He's just hanging in the water, watching us watching him."

I went and broke up the card game; O'Shea wasn't happy, as he'd been losing badly and wanted to win back his losses. He'd also been at the drink, I could smell it on him, and that usually spelled trouble. But he backed off when I mentioned that we had company. I sent Bailey and Kaminski up top to lay out the lines for the harpoon balloons we'd managed to retrieve from our last kill and sent O'Shea off to get the AUV back in the water, but only after checking he wasn't too drunk to get the job done. I asked Geordie to get a couple of depth charges ready. He had been on the booze too, but the whisky and him were old pals and I knew he could handle it; we'd had too much practice together over the years. He came with me as far as the bridge door but wouldn't come in.

"Lovers' tiff?" I asked with a grin, but didn't get a smile in return.

"Aye. And it's your fault, boss. I told her off for telling you to fuck off."

"What did she say to that?"

"What do you think? She told me to fuck off."

Moira still had an eye on the radar when I went inside.

"Is the big lad still there?"

"Same place, boss."

"Okay, let's see what kind of dance he's after. Get us underway and turn us round to face him. Don't get any closer; just turn us round."

"You have a plan, boss?"

"Might do. Let's just see what he does first. How deep is it around here?"

"Too deep for the same trick that got the other one, that's for sure," Moira replied. "There's more than a hundred feet of water below us right now."

"Plan B it is then. Softly goes it. I just want to let him know we're onto his game."

"And what if he wants us to know he's onto ours?"

"Then the dance really gets going."

Moira brought us round so smoothly I would hardly have noticed it had happened if I wasn't expecting it, and two minutes later the beastie and *The Havenhome* were facing each other down with only a hundred yards of open water between us. He didn't seem to be showing any interest in us, but my gut was telling me a different story.

"Did Geordie get the charges ready?"

Moira nodded.

"Only thing he's done right all day."

"Good. And Ruru will be ready, he's always ready. Is the AUV in the water?"

"Aye. It's behind us right now, just starting a wide circle. Its path will take it just in front of your pal in about two minutes."

"Then we wait. See who blinks first."

"If you want to know who shits themselves first, that'll be me," Moira said.

"Too late," I replied. "I win."

- 11 -

Two minutes felt like a lifetime and the tension would have had even Clint Eastwood squinting. Once again Moira provided a countdown, this time of the AUV's approach distance to our quarry.

"Fifty yards and our lad hasn't so much as twitched yet."

I was doing enough twitching for both of us, and I had to steady my hand to get a cigarette lit; I knew we were working on razor-fine margins here, and the line between a successful hunt and a full on calamity was going to be a difficult one to walk.

"Forty yards," Moira said.

"Move us closer," I replied. "Full throttle. And keep a finger on the depth charges button."

"Thirty yards. And our lad's moving. Heading towards the bot."

"Keep straight at him," I said, aware that I was almost shouting. At the same time I was doing frantic mental calculations; I could see the scenario in 3D in my head. It was going to be tight, and the whole thing depended on the beastie going for the bot rather than coming for us. I sent up a silent prayer to the gods of drunken sailors.

"Fifteen yards. He's definitely after the bot."

"Right at him," I replied then, a second later, "Drop the charge and hard a'port."

Moira hit the button and spun the wheel; there was a thunk from the back end as the depth charge was released. I counted out in my head from five down to one and got there as our whole rear end rose up and back down with a jarring crash that shook the boat from bow to stern. I held my breath, but none of the main alarms went off; at least the first of my numerous worries had been allayed.

I got out of the chair and headed for the foredeck, getting there just in time to see the harpoon line, inflating balloon attached, snake across the deck and over the side. Bailey and Kaminski were already loading a second harpoon. Beyond Ruru I saw the beast's tail fluke rise up as it dived, taking a mostly-inflated balloon down with it into the depths. My shout of triumph was quickly cut off. The balloon popped back up almost immediately, and beyond that the beast surfaced, took one look in our direction, then headed off at speed off to the north, soon to be lost in the near-darkness of approaching night.

I had Bailey and Kaminski retrieve the balloon and went to talk to Ruru.

"Did he seem at all damaged by the charge?" I asked.

He shook his head.

"Not that I could see. It brought him to the surface long enough for me to try to stick him, but like the female, his skin's too tough. I'm not getting any penetration."

"You and me both," Geordie said at my back before addressing me.

"O'Shea is below calling you nasty names, lad. The old girl took a good rattling but the hull held. We're all in one piece, but he doesn't recommend pulling that stunt again."

Moira called out from the bridge.

"Something you should see, boss."

The main console monitor in the bridge showed a still picture that had come in from the AUV just before the charge blew. All that could be seen was a gaping mouth, twin rows of fang-like teeth that filled the screen.

There were no more pictures transmitted.

We found what was left of the bot five minutes later; it looked even worse than before and O'Shea swore long and loud before taking the various bits below to his workshop.

"Do you think he's still watching us?" Geordie asked as we had a smoke by the bridge door. Bailey and Kaminski had got the balloon back aboard and deflated and we had two lines set out in case Ruru got another shot at the big lad. We had two depth charges…our last two… hooked up to the rig at the stern, and I had the big floodlight on, pointed behind and starboard at our lad's seemingly favored position. But there had been no sign, or radar contact, since our last encounter.

I'd taken so long answering Geordie I wasn't sure he was expecting one, but the same thought had been on my mind anyway.

"Aye, Geordie. He's watching us, and we're watching out for him. Ruru thinks we've got some psychic bond thing going on; his ancestors tell him we're connected."

"Aye? Well his ancestors can get tae fuck. Last time they told him anything it was that Moira and I were destined for each other for eternity. Funny story, eh? I cannae even get her tae look at me these days."

"She'll come around."

"Aye. And so will Christmas, but I gave up believing in Santa a wee while ago."

Between the two of us this kind of rapid descent into the maudlin usually ended at the bottom of a whisky bottle, but I couldn't afford to indulge that craving right then. I saw over Geordie's shoulder that Ruru had straightened and tensed at the harpoon station; that level of alertness only meant one thing, and Moira confirmed it at my back.

"We've got a ping, boss. Same place, same distance as before. Shall I turn us around to face him again?"

"No, not this time," I said loud enough for her to hear. "We don't have the bot to lure him with any more. We need a different strategy."

"Whatever you're thinking of, make it fast; he's not hanging about. Circling around off the starboard side now."

I peered off into the dark to starboard but it was a cloudy night and all I saw was the dark shards of some volcanic islands, blacker shadow against shadow. But the rocks got me thinking, of legends, of psychic bonds between lovers and my brain made connections I didn't know were possible until the idea came to me.

"Sirens," I said out loud.

"I don't hear any alarm, boss," Geordie replied, looking at me as if I'd just gone mad.

"No, not that kind. The Greek kind. We ken the big lad likes to dance. I wonder how he feels about a wee song?"

I hurried into the bridge and told Moira what I wanted. Two minutes later a wail went out over the tannoy above the deck and howled across the dark sea; the hydrophone recording of what we presumed had been the big lad's mate.

The result was immediate. I'd been hoping to lure him in slowly by making him curious. All I had accomplished was to make him angry.

"He's coming right at us, boss. Two hundred yards, one fifty. Oh fuck."

"I get the message. Hard left and drop a charge."

"But…"

"Do it. Right fucking now."

Instinct and training kicked in and Moira did as she was told, which was the only chance we had in the next few seconds. The howl on the tannoy was answered from somewhere out in the dark; I took that as a good sign for it meant he was at the surface and if Ruru could see him there was more than a chance we'd get through this.

"He's right on us," Moira shouted.

Then the charge went off. I left my chair as if someone had pushed an ejector seat button, my head hit a ceiling that had been five feet above my head a second earlier and it was lights out for me as I went down to a dark place where dead sailors still screamed and ravenous beasts waited.

- 12 -

I came out the dark into too much light with the taste of smoke and whisky in my mouth and Moira's face looming over me. It took a second or two for me to focus and when I managed it, I realized I was lying on the bridge floor staring at a ceiling where a layer of blue smoke hung just below the strip lighting. Our fire alarm was blaring but I guessed that wasn't terminal, given that both Moira and Geordie were still here on the bridge.

"Did we get the fucker?" I managed to say, although every word brought a drumbeat in my forehead, which felt too large, too tight. And I saw the answer in Moira's face, so I went on. "How bad is it?"

"We were taking on water for a wee while," Geordie said, "But O'Shea got the bilge pumps working in time, I helped him weld up a cracked seam, and we're on an even keel. She'll need some work when all's said and done though."

"Everybody okay?"

"Apart from you, aye. You've had a bad dunt on the head. Just lie there a bit, make sure it's no' concussion."

"It's nothing a few drams will no' fix," I replied. I craned my head and saw that the blue smoke was coming up from the galley below. "And the fire?"

"Electrical blow-out. In Stevie's domain. She's well pissed off, she's lost the contents of the big pantry, but she's not hurt; Kaminski got the extinguisher on it before it spread too far."

"Are we seaworthy?"

"Aye, boss. The engines still run just fine, no thanks to you. The back end might be bent a wee bit out of shape but it adds character."

"And the beastie?"

"He gave us a good hard Glesga kiss at the same time the charge went off, then he buggered off again right sharpish," Geordie replied. "Ruru tried to stick him but couldnae get a clear shot at the eye; he thinks that might be the only way to take this fucker down."

"I think I might agree with him on that," I replied. "Either that or putting one right down his gullet, but I don't fancy having to get that close again."

I went to sit up but Moira pushed me back.

"Just lie there and do what you're telt for once, would you?"

"On one condition," I said.

"What's that, boss?"

"Give me a fag. I'm gasping here."

With the aid of some more whisky and a smoke I was able to get up into my chair a few minutes later, but the effort that took told me I wasn't in any condition to be doing any running around for a while. The drumbeat in my head was incessant and when I felt around there appeared to be a heavy egg above my left eye that was tender to the touch. At least the fire alarm had been quietened, but the lights seemed too bright, searing diamond-like flickers into my retinas when I looked up.

"There's been nothing on the radar?" I said to Moira.

"Bugger all," she replied. "But I don't think it's because he's feert of us. Oh, and by the way, I turned the tannoy off… I don't think he liked it."

"I wasnae too keen on it myself."

"Why did he react like that to it? Any idea, lad?" Geordie said. He was taking advantage of his being allowed to be present on the bridge but even in my slightly befuddled state I noticed that he and Moira still weren't exactly on speaking terms.

"Not a Scooby, pal," I answered. "But if I had to hazard a guess, what we've got recorded there is a pregnant female, possibly in distress. We pushed all his protective father buttons at the one time, and you saw the result as well as I did,"

"Let's no' do that again, eh?"

"I'm in no hurry to try. Are we going anywhere or are we at anchor?"

"Still in the same place we were when we took the hit," Moira replied, "and waiting instructions."

"Get us the fuck out of here," I said. "Somewhere shallow and calm where I can get my head screwed on again."

"Yes, sir," Mora replied with a mock salute. "Fucking off commencing."

I sat back in my chair and closed my eyes, then immediately opened them again as a wave of nausea washed through me and the drumbeat threatened to send me back down to darkness.

"How're you feeling, lad?" Geordie asked.

"Like hammered shite," I replied. "How about you?"

"Same as it ever was," Geordie replied, and not for the first time he addressed it to Moira's back rather than to me. "I'll go check on O'Shea, make sure that weld's holding. Be back in ten."

I managed to focus on my watch and was surprised to see it was only nine o' clock; it felt like an eternity had passed since sundown, but the night was still young. I shouted after Geordie.

"Swing by my cabin and fetch yon bottle of the good stuff and another packet of fags," I replied. "It could be a long night."

The blue smoke above had all dissipated but I could still taste it in my throat.

"Any chance of a coffee?" I said to Moira. Stevie's muffled voice came up from below.

"Coming right up, boss. Good to hear you're back with us."

I felt better immediately just hearing her voice.

"I took your advice and fucked off," I shouted down. "Might have taken it a bit far though."

"Come down when you're up to it," she replied, "And I'll make it up to you."

In my current condition I knew I wasn't up to any kind of 'making up' that might be in Stevie's thoughts, but it made me feel even better just thinking about it, and when the coffee arrived it helped too. By the time Geordie turned up with the whisky and smokes I was feeling much more like my old self.

Moira brought us round a headland and into an empty crescent bay below a row of volcanic peaks. We dropped anchor in twenty feet of water a hundred yards offshore and slowly the boat went quiet around us. She felt wrong to me, injured in some way as if I could sense her distress. I had Geordie pour the three of us a stiffener and we had a toast to *The Havenhome,* after which I felt better about the state of her. We're a superstitious lot, we sailors and although we practice stoicism in the main, we can also get sentimental about the least wee thing. Tonight was one of my sentimental nights.

We all kept an eye on the radar, waiting for a blip that didn't come, and we spoke of old times. Two whiskies even softened Moira up enough to at least allow her to endure Geordie's presence by her side, and that seemed to be enough for my old friend. Times like this is what strengthens friendships built on mutual hardships and despite my thumper of a headache, it's been added to my short list of happy memories with good people.

We brought the night to an end somewhere around midnight, our quiet being disturbed by ructions downstairs; O'Shea and the two deck hands had gone back to their card game, and from the sound of it, O'Shea was losing again, badly and noisily.

I made to get out of the chair, and the world span alarmingly around me. Geordie patted me on the shoulder.

"I'll handle it, boss. Should have told them to pack it in earlier."

I saw Moira look as Geordie left.

"He's a good friend," I said.

"Aye. I ken that. But we make lousy lovers."

I had no answer to that one. In fact, I had no answer to much of anything. The night, and the whisky finally caught up with me and sleep hit before I even knew it was coming. The last thing I remember is Moira draping an overcoat over me, and then I was gone to dreamland where, thankfully, none of my demons were waiting for me.

- 13 -

I came out of sleep with a start, and this time the piercing light wasn't from the strip lighting but from morning sun streaming in the window of the bridge. I smelled coffee, put out a hand and as if by magic a mug was put in my palm.

"Morning, boss," Moira said. "How you doing now?"

I squinted against the light, but there were none of the diamond flickers from the night before and although my head hurt as if it had been pounded long and hard, the drumbeat was down to a manageable drone. I stood, gingerly, and felt none of last night's dizziness or nausea.

"I guess I'll live," I said. I pointed at the console. "Any sign?"

She knew what I was asking.

"Not a sausage. Might be we're too shallow for him, might be we scared him off."

"And might be he's just outside our range, waiting for us to make a move."

"Ruru's at the harpoon station," Moira said. "He's been there since sun-up. He'll let us know if there's anything in the area. You got a plan?"

"Breakfast, a smoke and a wee walk on deck to clear the head."

"Sounds like a good plan to me. I'll be here when you need me."

"Did you sleep?"

"Caught a couple of hours while you were out. Dinna fash… just get your head right, that's the main thing."

A rib-busting hug and a plate of ham and eggs from Stevie did a lot to set me back on track, although someone seemed to be moving the stairs to the upper deck when I left the galley to go topside. Fresh air hit me and threatened to knock me on my arse, but I stiffened my back, lit a smoke, and walked over to Ruru trying to look as if I was in charge of the situation.

He looked me up and down and laughed out loud.

"You should be in your bed. A stiff breeze will blow you down out here, the state you're in."

"I look that good, huh?"

"I've seen you better."

"And you've seen me worse. Remember yon night in Rio?"

He laughed again.

"I do. I had to carry you for two miles before we found a taxi. But that was self-inflicted."

I touched my bruised head and winced.

"So is this, in a way. Geordie tells me you couldn't get a clean shot?"

He nodded.

"The charge went off, he came up to the surface but the boat was heaving too much below me; I missed."

"I bet your ancestors weren't happy about that."

He looked glum.

"Them and me both. I just need one good clear look at him, and we'll have him. Can you get me a clear shot, boss?"

"I intend to try, lad. I intend to try."

My next call was to O'Shea and the deck hands. I apologized for getting the old girl in trouble, they apologized for the noise during their card game and I inspected O'Shea and Geordie's new weld in the foredeck cargo area. There was still some water sloshing about underfoot and it looked like it had got to a couple of feet deep at one point judging by the water damage to some of the crates.

"How close were we to going down?" I asked.

O'Shea smiled.

"Don't know, boss. I was busy getting wet. If I had to guess, maybe five more minutes and we'd have been in serious trouble. But Geordie and I handled it just fine. No sweat."

I didn't believe that for a minute, but I appreciated his effort to keep the details vague. It gave me less to worry about in the immediate future.

Final call before heading back to the bridge was on Geordie. I found him inspecting the damage at our rear end. The guard rail had been ripped from its moorings, leaving behind a line of ragged holes in warped deck plates. The depth charge housing had been on fire at some point, the metal blackened. Geordie was studying a charred circuit board.

"I believe the technical term is 'fucked'," he said. "We'll need to drop the next one manually… the last one I mean. We're down to thin rations, lad. If we don't get him next time, I doubt we'll be getting him at all."

"Ruru just needs one chance," I said.

"Don't we all?" he replied and not for the first time I was sure he wasn't talking about the Shonisaurus.

"There's another thing, boss," he said. "Didn't want to bother you with it last night after your bang on the head, but the wee nyaff fae the Yacht Club is still after you. The messages are piling up."

I decided that what would really clear my head would be to swear, long and loud, at someone. I returned to my cabin, lit a smoke and called up the yacht club on videocam.

He was where I expected him to be, behind the big desk, looking exactly like the smug wee git that he was.

"I've sent you more than a dozen messages… " he started.

"Aye. I've been ignoring them," I said, interrupting him. "What the fuck do you want?"

"I want a progress report."

"When we make any, you'll get one. I'll personally come over there and ram it up your arse."

"I'm not sure I like your tone."

"I'm not sure I give a fuck. I'm out here trying to catch a monster, you're back there being a fucking pencil-pushing money hugger. I think I've got the better deal, if you'll just leave me the fuck alone to get on with the job you're not paying me for."

"You'll get your money when the job's done."

"What, the last one, this one or the next one? Fuck off. I'm going to kill this beastie, you're going to pay me, then I never want to fucking see you again. Do we have a deal?"

"We have always had a deal, Mr. Seton. It's just that…"

I hung up on him, and took more than a little pleasure in doing so. In fact, I felt good enough that it was time to get back to work.

Past time.

- 14 -

The bridge was empty when I returned, the engines switched off and we bobbed at anchor in a calm, quiet bay. I found Moira out on the foredeck having a smoke and went to join her. The clouds were being burned off quickly and the deck had started to warm; in an hour or so it would be too hot to sit on but for now it seemed a pleasant way to pass a smoke break.

"I think I'm going to have to do something daft to get this bugger," I said.

"Well, we wouldn't want you breaking the habits of a lifetime, would we?"

"I need you on my side, lass," I said. "After that thing with the chopper…"

"All forgotten, boss. You did the right thing, eventually."

"Then why hold it against Geordie?"

She smiled.

"Because I like fucking with his head. And he likes me liking fucking with his head."

I laughed.

"I don't get it."

"Neither does Geordie," she replied. "At least not until he apologizes."

"And you've told him this?"

"Fuck, no," she said, laughing. "That's for me to know and him to find out."

"And Stevie? She's okay with me?"

"You need to ask her that yourself, boss. You're a big boy now, you can handle it."

"Which brings us back to me doing something daft," I replied. "Are you up for some more excitement?"

"Always."

"Come on then, finish the smoke. Let's go and see if the big lad wants a last dance."

"What's on your mind, boss?"

"A cunning plan. So cunning you could pin a tail on it and call it a fox."

All that got me was a blank look. Remember those cultural touchstones I was talking about?

Getting old sucks.

I called the crew together in the galley a few minutes later.

"You all know this isn't a democracy," I said. "But I'm giving you a chance to fuck off now if you want to. I'm going to do something stupid. And risky. And stupidly risky. And I'd hate for any of you to get hurt and to have it on my conscience."

"How risky are we talking?" O'Shea piped up. "Never living to see our pensions risky, or just losing the boat and never seeing a pension anyway risky?"

"Maybe neither, maybe both. I've got a plan."

"Is it cunning?" Geordie asked, and I smiled until I realized he was as old as me and suffering the same malady.

"You're fucking right it's cunning. But I don't even know if it's possible. I'm going to need some technical help."

"You know me, boss," O'Shea replied. "If there's a drink or a woman in it, I'm your man."

"All I can promise you is a trip to yon wee posh yacht club if we pull this off. The rest is up to you."

O'Shea threw me a mock salute. I looked around the others. Nobody seemed in a hurry to leave, so I continued.

"It was seeing the way the big lad came at the sound of the female that got me thinking," I said.

"Aye, that was something else, wasn't it," Geordie butted in. "I thought for a second he was going to try to hump us."

"Most action you've seen in a month," Moira replied, and I was only allowed to continue when the laughter died down.

"So he came to the sound," I said. "Maybe he'd do the same thing again. But I'm not about to put the boat at risk again like the last time; that was too close even for my liking. So what I want to know is, do we have the ability to transmit the noise at a distance...put a speaker underwater, rig it up to a charge, wait till he takes the bait, then blow him to fuckery?"

I saw that I'd got O'Shea thinking, and that fact alone was enough to give me hope. He piped up a few seconds later.

"If I can cannibalize the tannoy system?"

"Feel free."

"Then I think I can see how to do it. I'll need a couple of hours though?"

"Best get to it, then, lad. Any help you need, just shout. We're not going anywhere."

We didn't go anywhere as the sun passed overhead in a clear blue sky. It got warm... it got fucking warm, but at least no other boats turned up in the bay, neither leisure nor reporters. The wee nyaff in the yacht club stayed quiet too, which was something to be thankful for, and I spent the time getting my head screwed back on right, drinking coffee and smoking too many cigarettes.

Moira was at the con, still following the newsfeeds; they were still speculating about the loss of the chopper but nobody had drawn any real conclusions, and nobody mentioned us; our fifteen minutes of fame had already come and gone.

O'Shea came up on deck, and went back down to his work area again trailing a tannoy speaker, much wiring, and a circuit board from Moira's consoles that he said was 'redundant' and she said 'fucking better be.'

Stevie brought us up some omelets for lunch, and smiled at me as she left so I figured all was once again on an even keel on that side of things. Bailey and Kaminski were doing deckhand stuff, Geordie was helping O'Shea, and my only worry was Ruru, who was once again standing duty at the harpoon station, and once again not looking happy with his lot.

I pulled on a hat to shield my thinning pate from the sun and went out to see what was bothering him.

"It just doesn't feel right," he said as I handed him a smoke.

"Ancestors or gut?" I asked.

"I think both. The big booger is still out there watching us. I haven't seen him, but I know it, here," he tapped at his chest over his heart.

"I've been feeling the same way," I admitted. "We're not finished dancing with this guy yet."

"I'll mark his card for him," Ruru said as I turned to leave. "Just get me my clear shot."

I was aware my plan had too many moving parts, too many variables, but given the size of the beastie, the only way I knew to get us an advantage was to lure him into these shallow waters. After that, it was anybody's game.

O'Shea pronounced himself finished in the late afternoon and called us up on deck to show us a Heath-Robinson contraption of multiple propellers, cannibalized air tanks and a central body that I knew was our last depth charge that had a wee glass dome containing a speaker fitted on top of it, making it look like a squat robot from a Flash Gordon serial.

"Does it work?" Geordie asked.

"Well, I didn't want to test it," O'Shea said with a grin. "If it does work, yon big bugger is likely to come running, and I don't want it humping my leg." He turned to me. "The only test will be to get it in the water, back the fuck away from it, then switch it on."

"Sounds like a plan to me," I said. "Make it so. Good job."

It was, finally, show time.

- 15 -

While Bailey and Kaminski laid out the lines for the harpoon balloons, Geordie and I helped O'Shea put his contraption in the water, after which the Irishman handed me a wee box with two buttons, one green, one red.

"Green gets the song and dance started, red gets it finished with a bang," he said. "Don't get them mixed up."

We watched the bot descend until we could still just about see it, twelve feet or so down with the bottom shimmering about the same distance again below it.

"Unless there's a rip current we don't know about, it should stay there or thereabouts until you need it," O'Shea said. "When do we start?"

"I was thinking about now would be good," I replied, and headed back to the bridge.

"Back off fifty yards towards shore, and hold position," I said to Moira and she moved to comply immediately. Geordie had come with me and was standing just inside the door.

"If this doesn't work, he'll be right on top of us with no time for us to do anything about it."

"I know. I told you it was risky."

"Probably your stupidest idea yet, lad," he said.

"Nah. That was giving you a job," I replied.

"Fair enough," he said. "But are we going to stand around here flapping our lips or are you actually going to do something?"

I turned back to Moira.

"Are we in position?"

"Aye, boss."

"Then let's do this."

I pushed the green button.

I had been wondering whether we'd hear anything. Moira was ahead of me and switched on one of the hydrophones. The eerie wail we'd recorded from the female echoed around the bridge while Moira kept an eye on the radar.

"Do you think he'll come?" Geordie said.

"If he's in hearing range, he'll come. And I'm pretty sure he's in range; he's been keeping an eye on us all this time. I feel it in my bones."

My gut instinct was confirmed seconds later.

"We've got company. Starboard side, two hundred yards and closing."

I leaned back in my chair and looked out the door to the harpoon station. Ruru was at his post, staring off the starboard bow.

"This is it, folks. Moira, I need a distance countdown between the big lad and O'Shea's wee toy."

"On it, boss. He's heading right for it and coming on like a bullet. Ninety yards out. Eighty."

Once again, I could see it all in my head like a three-dimensional map. I waited until Moira's countdown reached ten, took a breath and hit the red button, praying that O'Shea hadn't fucked up.

The charge went up with a blast that shook the boat, and at the same time I was up and out of the chair heading out onto the deck.

The beast came out of the water head-first twenty yards off our starboard bow. His lower jaw hung loosely, only being held on by fragments of torn muscle and shattered bone, but there was still plenty of life in the big lad as he fixed his gaze on the boat and came on again, hard and fast. He was going to hit us almost exactly below where Ruru stood, but the harpoonist didn't flinch. He had already taken aim and fired when the beast was only three or four yards from impact. The harpoon didn't have far to travel. It went directly into the right eye and kept going until the whole length of it had disappeared, embedding itself in the thing's brain. The beastie hit us, but much of his momentum had now been dissipated and the jolt, while it rocked us, didn't topple us over.

The beast was surely fatally wounded, but it took him some time to realize it. He turned away, obviously intent on making an escape. The harpoon line snaked across the deck, the balloon already inflating. The beast bellowed in rage and pain, a wail every bit as eerie and terrifying as that made by the female. He rolled in the water, his good eye staring at me then, just as if a switch had been pulled, all the life went out of him and he began to sink.

"Get a line on him," I called to Ruru. "I don't want to lose him. The mannie at the yacht club won't be able to deny this."

The next half hour was rather frantic as we all helped reel the big bugger in and use the winches to get him hoisted up on deck, or at least, as much of him as we were able, for his heft and weight was such that he threatened to drag us down at the stern until I had Geordie lower his rear end back into the water. The engines strained at first when Moira got us going again, and I thought we might overheat, but finally we were underway, dragging most of the beastie behind us.

"What's the plan, lad?" Geordie said as we shared a smoke.

"We're making for the yacht club," I replied. "I want to look in the money man's face when he sees what he's bought."

- 16 -

It proved to be slow going. The extra weight at the back was doing nothing for our stability under power and Moira had her hands full keeping us on an even keel. The rest of us found ourselves continually drawn to the stern for a look at our catch. It was certainly worth looking at, even with its jaw blown to fuckery and back. There were still plenty of teeth on the upper set to impress us. Moira had estimated its length at almost eighty feet, and had been doing some research, trying to match our photos against artist's impressions in the online reference books.

"*Shonisaurus sikanniensis*," she said. "Or maybe *Shastasaurus*. It comes down to how slender the body and flippers are and…"

I tuned the rest of it out. As I've said already, I don't need to know their names, only how to kill them. And we'd done a bloody good number on this particular specimen.

We'd already taken scores of video clips and hundreds of photographs, although I had to warn the younger lads, Bailey and Kaminski, against sharing anything on their social media accounts.

"We don't want the press finding us before they have to," I said. "Although we're hardly inconspicuous dragging this big fucker around, I'd rather we flew under the radar as long as possible. Don't worry, once they get a gander at this lad, the press will be all over us for a while; you'll get another go at your fifteen minutes of fame."

My reasoning was that I didn't want to give Franks at the yacht club enough time to scupper my plans for a big entrance; I was looking forward to rubbing his nose in it. It might be the only chance I ever got.

On my fourth, maybe fifth, visit to the stern I found Ruru there. He wasn't looking at the dead beastie though; he had his gaze fixed some way off behind us, his hand raised to his brow to shield his eyes from the sun. I tried peering in that direction but all I saw was heat-haze and glare.

"What is it, lad? Trouble?"

"I don't know. At first I thought it was sharks, drawn by this dead thing, Now? I'm not so sure. Whatever it is, they're staying well back."

"Probably not sure enough that this fucker's dead; I would want to mess with it if I was in two minds about it."

He still frowned and went quiet, but he stopped me as I was about to leave.

"This isn't over, boss. Not by a long chalk."

Sometimes I wished his bloody ancestors would just shut the fuck up.

Our luck held for longer than I thought it might, and we were only a couple of miles from the entrance to the yacht club marina when the first chopper came by, circled for a good long look at us, then disappeared off at speed. Within ten minutes we had three choppers as accompaniment, the radio was constantly squawking for attention, and Moira was getting email alert pings every few seconds. I guessed my own inbox would also be filling up fast but I ordered everybody to ignore the cries for attention.

"We're delivering this cargo and nobody's going to stop us," I said over the con. Nobody tried to contradict me, a small mercy but one I was thankful for. I figured we were about to become the center of attention. It was time to do some grandstanding.

Minutes later we arrived at the mouth of the marina entrance to find a small flotilla of yachts, pleasure craft, dinghies and even rowing boats coming out to meet us. It became a procession behind us as Moira kept going on the heading I'd set her...directly for the main dock below Franks' office window.

For once he wasn't at his desk; he was down on the pier waiting for us to dock, and the look on his face was every bit as horrified as I'd hoped.

"What the blazes do you think you're doing?" were his first words to me after I had the gangplank lowered and stepped down beside him.

"One beast, as ordered," I said. "I consider this our contract fulfilled, and if you know what's good for you, so will you. Or shall I be the one to tell the story?"

I waved over his shoulder; three different film crews were heading towards us at a run. Maybe if he'd had time to develop countermeasures things might have gone differently, but at that moment I was holding all the cards, and he knew it.

"Keep your mouth shut and you'll be paid as soon as I get finished with these scum. Say a single word, and all deals are off."

I smiled, drew an imaginary zip across my lips, and waited for the wolves to descend on him.

To be fair to him he made a good fist of it, making a wee speech about how somebody had to take responsibility for ending the menace, and how he, reluctantly, had taken on that mantle. He even walked them along *The Havenhome* deck for some close ups of teeth and punctured eyeball. And when the wolves' attention inevitably turned to me, he expertly drew them back to himself, citing 'contractual obligations' and 'non-disclosure agreements.' They weren't happy about being fobbed off, but he had the advantage of home ground; that, and the growing presence of his security team around us were enough to ensure their compliance. They got what they needed for their prime-time reports, he got to bask in some unearned limelight, and I got to dream about counting my money.

As it turned out, the payment part was the easiest bit of the whole thing. He called up an app on his phone and with three finger-presses it was done. I looked up to the bridge where I knew Moira would be keeping tabs. She looked out, her grin wide, and gave me a thumbs-up.

Job done, time to dump our cargo and bugger off.

- 17 -

I was fully prepared to dump the carcass on the quay in front of the main yacht club building and was about to order Geordie and Ruru to get the process started when matters took an unexpected turn.

As you can probably imagine, it was quite noisy in the central part of the marina already, what with the choppers up above, the ever increasing number of gawkers on shore, and a growing flotilla of small vessels all jostling for a view of our catch.

The scream that came from the entrance to the marina from the open sea cut through all of that. I looked up, thinking that one of the smaller boats might have jostled a bit too vigorously and shipped a passenger or two. I was just in time to see the white sail of a dory get splashed with an inkblot splatter of blood.

Then the screaming really started. The water at the mouth of the marina foamed and roiled, white spume mixed with more red as small boats were toppled and their inhabitants were fed into the maws of whatever was ravening there. I couldn't take *The Havenhome* out to investigate; the inner marina was choked with boats, and getting busier all the time as the panicked flotilla tried to crowd in looking for safety. Beyond them the water churned and seethed. The smaller boats seemed to be being swallowed whole from below; one second they were there, the next there was nothing to be seen but debris and a hint of pink in the spume.

It was only when one of the bigger pleasure cruisers came under attack that I realized what was happening. The thing that came up out of the water was maybe half the size of the dead one draped over our stern, but it was still more than heavy enough to breach and come down fully across the superstructure of the cruiser, immediately swamping it and sending its quota of ten or more passengers down into the water.

None of them came back up.

I hadn't realized Ruru was by my side until he spoke.

"It's a pod, boss," he said. "And a big one; thirty or more, juveniles and females if I'm right."

"A pod? More like a fucking harem."

I couldn't draw my gaze away from the continuing carnage in the outer marina. Most of it was caused by rampaging beasts, but some, not a small amount, was due to the panicked efforts of too many boats to get into too small a space looking for an escape. Another ichthyosaur breached, the largest one yet, swamping one of the more expensive yachts, and I heard a muttered 'oh fuck' from one side. I turned to see Franks staring out aghast at the ruin of his wee empire. And all the while the news choppers fluttered overhead, their cameras soaking up the images for broadcast across the globe; there wasn't going to be any cover up of this story.

All I could do about it was stand and watch. It seemed to go on for hours but couldn't have been more than ten minutes, at the end of which the pod ghosted away as silently as they had come leaving behind an outer marina that was now little more than scattered debris.

I volunteered *The Havenhome*'s crew to help with the hunt for survivors and we took out our dinghies. It was a forlorn hope. Although numerous body parts were retrieved nobody came out of the carnage alive. As darkness was falling again, we returned to *The Havenhome* on the dock. Once again Franks was waiting for me.

"What the fuck are you going to do about this?" he screamed in my face.

"How is this my problem? It's your club. You fucking sort it out."

He waved at the carcass on *The Havenhome.*

"If you hadn't brought that here…"

"Me? You paid me to do it, remember? Tell you what, I'll take it off your hands, take it out to deep water and dump it. Then we'll call it quits. Deal?"

He had his phone out again.

"That's it. I'm canceling your payment."

I laughed in his face.

"Too late, old son. I had Moira transfer the money out as soon as it hit the bank. That ship has left port."

"Then I'll sue."

"Sue away. We had a contract, I fulfilled it. Twice. I'm happy to take my side of the case to court. Are you?"

I saw the bean counters at work in his head again, calculating odds and percentages. At first I was afraid he might call my bluff, but he wasn't as good with people as he was with money, and he backed down first.

He got out of my face and went back to staring out at the carnage.

"What can I do? What if they come back?"

"I've got some ideas about that," I said, and I saw hope in his eyes as he turned to me.

"Tell me," he said.

"Let's talk business," I replied.

- 18 -

I called a crew meeting ten minutes later in *The Havenhome*'s small mess area, and laid out what I'd just agreed with Franks.

"You did what?" Stevie said, almost a shriek.

"All of them?" Moira added.

"How much did you ask for?" Geordie, ever the pragmatist, asked.

"Five million pounds," I said. "And for that we take down the pod."

"Ballsy," O'Shea said.

"Fucking stupid," Stevie added.

"How, precisely, are you planning to go about it?" Moira asked.

I gave her my best smile.

"I just make the decisions," I said. "As for ideas? That's what I've got you lot for."

Nobody hit me, so I took that as a win and continued.

"Look, we already know how to attract them; yon recording of the pregnant one will get them all coming running. What with that, and the carcass we've got hanging off the back, we can lure them anywhere we want them. We can herd them into shallow water."

"Aye," Geordie said. "Then what?"

"As I said, I'm open to ideas. But first, we need to slip out of here in the dark and hope nobody follows us. Moira, can you get us out quietly, no lights showing?"

"Aye, I can do that. But what if yon pod is just waiting for us to do that very thing?"

"Then I'll need those ideas sooner rather than later."

Stevie cornered me at the galley door as we were preparing to slip away. She had a traveling bag over her left shoulder.

"This is as far as I go, John," she said.

"If this is about the thing with the chopper pilots…"

"It's about that, yes. But it's mostly about death. I've seen enough of it. These beasts are just doing what they do. And they're important, historically and scientifically. They should be protected, studied…"

"That's somebody else's job if they want to do it. I'm a hunter, Stevie. It's who I am, it's what I do. You knew the score when you signed on for the gig."

She touched my face, gently, far too sadly for my liking.

"Yes, you're a hunter all right, John Seton. You captured a part of me I didn't even know was there.

But now you should set me free. I don't have the heart, or stomach for it any more, if I ever had."

"What will you do?"

"What I've always done. Find somewhere to cook, and somebody that'll appreciate it."

"I appreciate it."

"Yes. But not enough. Goodbye, John. I'd wish you luck, but luck's never been your problem."

Before I could stop her, she'd kissed me lightly on the cheek and turned away, off, up the stairs and out of my life before I thought to ask her to stay.

"She's gone?" Moira asked as I arrived in the bridge a few minutes later.

"Aye. You knew?"

"She told me earlier. I tried to talk her out of it, but she had her mind made up."

"She'll be back," I said, trying to convince myself, but I could see from Moira's face I wasn't fooling anybody. I put it to one side, for now, knowing it was something I'd be returning to one of those dark nights when there was just me, a cigarette and a bottle. We had work to do, and serious money to be made, and it was time to get to it.

"Cast off at the sharp end," I said. "And take her out, nice and slow."

"Aye, aye, Captain," Moira said, getting in the spirit of things.

We left the marina under cover of darkness, running with no lights, and didn't hit anything on our way out. Nothing hit us either, which I suppose was something to be grateful for.

I'd asked for ideas. Geordie's one of 'fucking off home with the money we'd got already' certainly held its appeal, but five mill was a lot to think about; enough to fund us for years to come. I would be able to devote more time to looking for scar-eye without having to worry over duly about finding work. That too held its appeal.

I was surprised that Moira sided with Geordie when it came to taking the money and running, but I was determined to hold out for more than that. As such I was relieved when Ruru and O'Shea turned up on the bridge. By this time it was three in the morning, we were all running on fumes, Stevie wasn't there to keep the coffee coming, but the two men appeared excited at whatever it was they'd concocted.

"Spill it then, lads," I said. "This had better be good."

O'Shea did most of the talking.

"I was asking your man here about his ancestors, and an interesting point came up. He comes from a long line of hunters who live off the sea."

"Aye, I ken that already. Is there a point coming?"

"He was telling me a story about how they used to round up porpoise by herding them into a shallow bay, then club them to death. I remembered I'd seen the same thing done in the Faroe Islands, but with dolphins. We were thinking we might be able to do something along the same lines."

"Hit them with big sticks? That's your plan? Fucking brilliant. I wonder why I never thought of that myself."

Ruru surprised me by speaking up.

"It's a simple tactic, but it works, boss. And the Irishman here has some ideas that go beyond big sticks if you just hear him out."

Over the next twenty minutes I heard him out and I was so impressed I marched them both down to the mess and treated them to whisky and beer 'on the house'.

We had a plan.

- 19 -

The first stage of the operation was in two parts. Geordie and O'Shea were working on one part down in the workshop area. The sound of whatever they were doing echoed the length and breadth of the boat in a series of clangs and bashes that had me wondering if they weren't perhaps cannibalizing the hull.

Part two was more in my line. With Moira's help I set about looking for the ideal spot to lay our planned ambush. We had the charts laid out in front of us and we pored over them for more than an hour without much luck. Our criteria was that we needed an enclosed, shallow bay with a narrow entrance. There were plenty of shallow bays, but it was finding one where we could block any escape route for the beasts that was proving to be the biggest problem.

It was only when I stopped looking for uninhabited spots that we made the breakthrough. Miller's Yacht Club had been a thriving concern once upon a time; I'd even had a beer or three in their bar many years ago. Now it was abandoned and derelict, its joys of a simpler age overtaken by the conspicuous debauchery on show in the more modern, larger marinas. Miller's time had long passed. But once I found it on the map and remembered the layout, I knew it would be almost perfect for our needs. The only problem was it was a solid three hours sail away at our current speed which was still being hampered by the carcass draped over our stern. But I couldn't dump it; it too was part of the plan that was unfolding in my mind in ever increasing detail. I could see how it could work in theory. In practice, again, it had a lot of moving parts, any one of which could fuck up the whole show. But the crew were on it, and I was dog-tired.

I retired to my cabin, got my head down and fell asleep to the arhythmic hammering and banging from O'Shea's workshop that showed no sign of slacking.

Thin early morning sun was coming in the porthole when I woke to an almost silent boat. I got some coffee from a pot someone had made earlier in the galley, looked for breakfast before I remembered Stevie wasn't aboard, and headed up top to catch up on what was going on. I saw that I'd risen just in time; we were approaching the opening that led into the old yacht club. Ruru and the deck hands were working on our large net; we hadn't used it for a while so I knew he was checking it for holes. There was no clanging from below, and when I reached the bridge I found Geordie and O'Shea there in conference with Moira.

"Are we ready?" I asked.

"As we'll ever be, boss," O'Shea said. "Can I run through it again; I just want to make sure it all makes sense in the cold light of day."

I waved him on. He counted down the actions on his fingertips, from getting the net ready in the mouth, setting out the hydrophones that had been fitted with the last of the tannoy speakers, the proposed weaponry which he'd laid out at the stern, and everybody's jobs that needed to be done if the trap was going to be sprung. It all still made sense to me. Then again, I wasn't going to be out in a dinghy on open water with a pod of hungry dinosaurs on my arse. That was O'Shea's job, and I could see it had him twitchy.

"I'll do it if you'd rather not," I said. "I'm just going to be mostly sitting on my arse in here anyway."

"After that bang on the head you took the last time? No. My idea, my job," he said. "Just remember your promise; dancing girls and all the booze I can swallow…"

"...and a new AUV on top. Aye. You can hold me to it if this caper works."

It was time to see if his planning matched his enthusiasm. O'Shea took me out on deck and showed me what they'd been working on through the night; it was a set of portable harpoon guns for four of us, compressed air driven from a cylinder to be strapped to your back and half a dozen vicious looking, heavy, barb-tipped spears for each of them.

"We've got these, we've got the net, and we've got Ruru on the big harpoon. If that's not enough, we're fucked," O'Shea said.

"Then we'd better make sure it's enough."

Ruru gave the big net his sign of approval. I say big… it was a drift net at the small end of the scale for them, only a hundred yards in depth but hopefully more than enough for our purposes here. I'd caught sharks with it in the past, although they'd been minnows compared to the job I was asking it to do today. It only needed to work once, and only for a few minutes. If it couldn't do that then, to quote my engineer, we were indeed fucked.

We hung the net off the bow as O'Shea readied the dinghy. Geordie was already in the second dinghy which was loaded with the modified hydrophones. Once O'Shea was ready, I had Moira take *The Havenhome* into the bay. The dinghies stayed at the mouth and, as soon as we were inside, Geordie and O'Shea began getting the net anchored to the rocks of the northern lip; the sound of the nail gun hammering pitons into the stone echoed all around the inner bay like gunshots.

The first part of my job in all of this was the easiest one. I had Moira take us all the way up to the rotting quay of the old yacht club, tied up on the port side, and dumped the big lad's carcass in the shallows off our starboard side. While we were doing that, Geordie's dinghy came back into the bay and made a semi-circle up close to the hull while he dropped the modified hydrophones. As he was doing that, I had Bailey and Kaminski don their harpoon backpacks and sent them up to the bow. Ruru had the starboard side. Geordie and I had agreed to take the other two spear guns and cover the rear, but Moira had other ideas. She left the bridge ahead of me and by the time I reached her she was already buckling on a tank.

"I'm no' a wee lassie to be left simpering while the men do the dirty work; you ken me better than that. You and Geordie can fight over who gets to play with the other one."

I knew better than to even try to argue and reached to lift the last tank. My head spun and a wave of dizziness ran over me.

"Leave it for Geordie, boss. You're no' fit for it."

I made a second reach for the tank with the same results as the first time. If I pulled rank here and forced the issue, I was liable to cock up and put everybody's life at risk. I had enough on my conscience without adding more. I gave in to the inevitable and when Geordie climbed aboard I let him take the last gun.

As for me, I returned to the bridge; at least there was a chance I might be of some use there. I looked forward and made out O'Shea standing at the mouth of the bay waving his arms in the air. He had one end of the net anchored.

All that was left now was to get the party started.

- 20 -

We were using the same button as before. I shouted out, "Game on," and hit the green button. This time I heard it, faint as if coming from a great distance, but a most definite, recognisable, high wail. O'Shea had set up four hydrophones to transmit simultaneously, in the hope the more the merrier, and also hoping that multiple sources might confuse the pod and give us an advantage.

The blips showed up on the radar almost immediately, a close group of them already closing in on where I gauged the bay mouth to be. This was a tricky moment for O'Shea out there alone in his dinghy. He had to wait for the pod to enter the bay before making a move to block any escape with the net. I tried to keep one eye on the radar and the other out the window to my view of the entrance. I counted down distances in my head.

They're inside the bay by now. They must be.

O'Shea was obviously of the same opinion; I saw the dinghy move north to south across the bay mouth and even from the distance I could see he dragged something heavy in the water behind him. The bait had been taken and the trap was closing.

The pod was moving fast, headed directly for us, so I had to turn my attention away from O'Shea, trusting that he'd get his end of the job done and anchor the net at the southern end.

"We've got incoming," I shouted, just as the first ichthyosaur broke the surface thirty yards off our bow. It was smaller than the two we'd already killed, but not by all that much, maybe forty to forty-five feet long and coming at us like a torpedo. I lost sight of it as it closed, lost below the bow rail, and saw Kaminski raise his harpoon gun, which suddenly didn't look nearly as formidable, then had to brace myself in the chair as a jolt shook the boat and threatened to knock me to the floor.

Both Bailey and Kaminski were now standing right at the bow rail, shooting down into the water below. I went out on deck in time to see Ruru put a harpoon down the gullet of a twenty-footer and marveled, not for the first time, at his composure as he reloaded and was ready to aim again within seconds.

Another jolt hit us, at the stern this time. The carcass of the dead one lay all along our exposed starboard side, serving as a barrier against attack that was, so far at least, proving to be effective. I'd tried to get the stern in between two wharves but it had been too tight and as such the back end was slightly exposed to the open water. It was as if the pod knew it; they were focussing an attack there, and Moira and Geordie had their hands full.

We took another hit, a hard one, as I was making my way to the stern. I managed to keep my feet. Geordie didn't. He stumbled, tried to correct himself, failed due to the weight of the tank on his back and went tumbling through a gap in the rail. Moira's wail rang out above the commotion. I ran over to her side. We both looked down to see Geordie sitting legs akimbo, on the tail fluke of the carcass, aiming between his feet at a ten-footer that was trying to come up out of the water after him. He put a harpoon into its head and it fell away. It was dead as it rolled back into the water, and deader still when a fifteen-footer dived in and tore a chunk as big as a barrel out of it. The waters in front of the carcass were a seething, roiling hubbub of flume, tinged pink with the blood of the beasts where they tore themselves apart in a feeding frenzy.

"Bloodlust," I shouted. "Don't bother trying for kill shots; just get the blood flowing. They'll do the rest themselves."

The sea turned red all around us, filled with guts and torn rags of skin, snapping teeth and thrashing tails. An acrid stench hung in the air and I realized I now understood Stevie a bit better; it was hard enough for a blood-soaked old hunter like me to see. If she'd had to look at this it would have broken her.

The feeding frenzy continued. Up high on the starboard side harpoon station Ruru picked the beasts off coldly and clinically, like hitting triple twenty at darts with every shot. Geordie didn't appear to be in any danger where he was and Moira was doing a good job of covering him from above, so I headed up front to check on the others.

Kaminski was down, sitting with his back against the port-side rail, his tank and weapon by his side. Blood ran down his face from what, on closer inspection, looked to be a scalp wound. His eyes were clear when he looked up at me.

"Busted my ankle at that last big dunt," he said. "Knocked me arse over tit. Sorry, boss."

I clapped him on the shoulder, and took up his cylinder and weapon. A fresh wave of dizziness threatened to topple me but pig-ignorant determination kept me upright long enough to step over and join Bailey at the rail. We had two harpoons each left…and nothing to shoot at. The water around us quietened until there was only the lap of red waves on the hull. The bay was filled with carcasses and pieces of carcasses and nothing moved except for Geordie, who was being helped back aboard at the rear by Moira and Ruru.

I looked out towards the mouth of the bay, looking for the Irishman. And that's when I saw it, halfway between us and the exit; a tail fluke, a large one, rose up and slapped the water three times, as if to challenge us.

The dance wasn't over yet.

- 21 -

O'Shea was okay. He was out of the dinghy…and out of harm's way, up on the rocks above the southern lip of the mouth, and already clambering over them heading back towards us.

Ruru had also moved; he'd seen the slaps of the tail fluke and was now back at his harpoon post having reloaded the weapon. I couldn't see any spares in the quiver at his side; he was down to his last shot. I realized I could still hear the wail from the hydrophones. I took out the transmitter and hit the red button. The bay fell silent.

Geordie, none the worse for wear, arrived at my side. I saw that he and Moira were holding hands, but didn't so much as smile…I didn't want to ruin their moment in case they hadn't actually noticed yet.

"So what now, lad? Is yon big bugger the only one left?"

"Sure looks that way," I replied. "He's stuck in here with us…"

"...and we're stuck in here with him," Moira finished for me.

"We have one advantage. If he makes a run for open water, he'll get caught in the net and we'll have him."

Moira gazed out across the red-tinged water.

"I think they're too smart for that," she said softly. "Much too smart."

As if to punctuate that, the tail fluke came up and slapped down, twice, before it went quiet again.

O'Shea arrived back minutes later, making his way gingerly along the rotted dock at our port side.

"Did we get them all?" he asked. "I mean, apart from the big fucker."

"If they all came into the bay, we got them," Moira said. "But I'd better check the radar, just in case."

I sent Geordie up to the bow where Bailey was tending to Kaminski, and went to join Moira on the bridge. There was only one blip on the radar, directly between us and the exit, and he was just hanging there, as if daring us to come for him. A sixty-footer if my guess was right. More than big enough to give us serious trouble.

Come and get me... if you've got the balls for it.

I had the balls for it all right. What I was lacking was the necessary big stick.

"I'm open to suggestions," I said a few minutes later. We were all out on deck, even Kaminski, who had a badly sprained ankle and a newly-bandaged head but apart from that appeared to be none the worse for wear. The big ichthyosaur was still, according to the radar, in the same spot, still just hanging there. There was no other movement in the bay, but there was going to have to be soon for the heat of the day was bringing a truly disgusting stench up from the offal in the waters around us. I lit a smoke to try to counter the smell. It almost worked.

"What have we got left?" Geordie asked.

"I've got one shot," Ruru said, "But that's all I'll need if we can get him to do what we want."

Geordie piped in.

"We've got seven spears for the air guns," he said. "And that's our lot."

"Not quite," I replied and turned to O'Shea.

"How much spare fuel are we carrying?"

"Twenty barrels," he said without even having to think about it. "What are you thinking? We can't blow them underwater… wouldn't work."

"I was thinking more along the lines of napalm," I replied, and saw by the slow grin that appeared on O'Shea's face that it might just be possible.

"That's all well and good, boss," Moira said once she'd understood my thinking, "But how do we get him to come up? I don't think the hydrophone trick will work again; we've overplayed that hand."

"We invite him to dance," I said. "And we ask nicely. It's time for another one of those Mexican standoffs you enjoyed so much the last time. But first, get us on the move before I boak."

By the time we left the dock, O'Shea and Geordie had already started pouring what the Irishman was calling his ju-ju juice off our back end. The propellers churned up a scum of bloody ichthyosaur parts and gore which got mixed in along with the oil and soap and we left a bloody, greasy trail behind us as I had Moira criss-cross the whole inner end of the small bay.

The beastie just sat there, still between us and the bay mouth. He wasn't moving, but I knew he was watching. I had Moira stop crossing the bay and turn us head on towards him. Geordie and O'Shea were still pouring the goop out the back end. They had two barrels left. I'd already told Geordie my plan, and I knew that he was ready to do his bit when the time came.

"Time to dance," I said and hit the green button on the wee transmitter, and at the same time calling out to Moira, "Hit it. Ramming speed."

I couldn't hear the hydrophones above the sound of the engines, but I did hear the hiss and whoosh as Geordie sent a flare high above the bay to let it fall into the center of the spilled fuel and soap. *The*

Havenhome flew forward as the fires of hell roared up high at our backs.

"He's coming right at us," Moira said. "Fifty yards. Forty."

I'd played games of chicken before, but none for such high stakes. For the next few seconds my heart was in my mouth. The bridge took on a red glare from the fire outside.

"He's right on us," Moira shouted and I braced myself, but the jolt never came; I'd out-bluffed him and he'd veered aside at the end, coming up off our starboard bow where Ruru was waiting for that very thing.

I got out on deck in time to see the harpoon take the beast in the eye. It didn't penetrate all the way, getting stuck on bone on the way in, but it was enough to distract the beast just long enough for it to barrel right into the heart of the flames at our bow, flames which were still being stoked by Geordie and O'Shea. They poured the last of the last barrel over the beast's back as we passed it.

A wild howl pierced the air and the beast turned. For a bad second I thought it was coming at us, then, still flaming, it was away and headed for the bay mouth. It hit the net full on, thrashing wildly like a hooked salmon, twisting and turning until the net was wrapped tight and burning along with the rest.

It took a while to die. Moira couldn't watch and I didn't much blame her, but I stood up on the deck for a while taking video and pictures. The money man would need them.

- 22 -

There was a hell of a mess to clear out of the way before we left the bay, and our wee fire party had burned down what little was left of Miller's Yacht Club, but the sharks were already moving in on the leftovers and the sea tends to its own; the next time I pass that way I doubt there'll be any sign of our wee fracas.

As I imagined, Franks huffed and puffed over paying me when we got back to the yacht club but softened when I gave him all the pictures and video. I even signed another agreement, no skin off my nose, not to talk to the press.

We got back underway after a two day furlough for the crew. I'd spent much of it looking for Stevie but she'd already moved on.

At least I was able to keep my promise to O'Shea. I left him in the yacht club with a bevy of girls and a large tab behind the bar.

In the morning he pronounced himself happy, although it was afternoon before I could get any work out of him.

The End

@severedpress
/severedpress

Check out other great

Sea Monster Novels!

Michael Cole

MEGALODON VS COLOSSAL SNAKE

Brought to life by the miracle of DNA cloning, a 93-foot Megalodon shark has escaped captivity. With an insatiable appetite and unmatched aggression, it travels west for the Georgia coast, leaving a path of destruction in its wake. Bullets and harpoons can't penetrate it, steel nets can't hold it, and it's only a matter of time before the whole world finds out about it. In a race to stop the beast, the organization responsible recruit a marine biologist and a herpetologist to develop a plan to catch it. To do it, they must unleash the company's other genetically modified experiment—a 150-foot snake, resurrected from the DNA of the mighty Titanoboa. The pursuit leads to inevitable combat, and the scientists are forced to witness the deadly realities of genetic tampering. As the battle escalates, it is clear nobody is safe...and that nature never intended for these beasts to return. As the destruction mounts, and the death toll climbs, the true loser of Megalodon vs. Colossal Snake is humanity.

Tim Waggoner

TEETH OF THE SEA

They glide through dark waters, sleek and silent as death itself. Ancient predators with only two desires – to feed and reproduce. They've traveled to the resort island of Las Dagas to do both, and the guests make tempting meals. The humans are on land, though, out of reach. But the resort's main feature is an intricate canal system . . . . . . and it's starting to rain.

Check out other great

Sea Monster Novels!

Edward J. McFadden III

SHADOW OF THE ABYSS

Out of the past comes an immense horror. An ancient creature that must feed its voracious hunger.A massive landslide on Grand Bahama Bank sends a thirty-foot wave traveling at 150MPH toward the east coast of Florida, and the tsunami drags in something horrible from the depths of the Mid-Atlantic Ridge rift valley. Now a monster roams Florida's east coast and its shallows, searching for prey.Matthew "Splinter" Woods lives in Sailfish Haven. He's a washed-out Navy SEAL who lives off the grid on his dilapidated boat and has withdrawn from society rather than face his demons. But when his ex-girlfriend, charter boat captain Lenah Brisbee, comes to him for help, Splinter gets drawn into a battle that pits him against the strongest enemy he's ever faced as he races against time to find the monster before it turns the waters he loves blood red.

Eric S. Brown

PIRANHA

The rains came, flooding the sleepy, little town of Sylva. Sheriff Hanson never thought that he would be fighting a battle to survive against real life monsters. . .but with the waters came flesh eating, hungry creatures that swept through Sylva's streets like locusts, devouring everyone in their path.

Check out other great

Sea Monster Novels!

Robert J. Stava

NEPTUNES RECKONING

At the easternmost end of Long Island lies a seaside town known as Montauk. Ground Zero on the Eastern seaboard for all manner of conspiracy theories involving it's hidden Cold War military base, rumors of time-travel experiments and alien visitors... For renowned Naval historian William Vanek it's the where his grandfather's ship went down on a Top Secret mission during WWII code-named "Neptune's Reckoning". Together with Marine Biologist Daniel Cheung and disgraced French underwater explorer Arnaud Navarre, he's about to discover the truth behind the urban legends: a nightmare from beyond space and time that has been reawakened by global warming and toxic dumping, a nightmare the government tried to keep submerged. Neptune's Reckoning. Terror knows no depth

Bestselling collection

DEAD BAIT

A husband hell-bent on revenge hunts a Wereshark... A Russian mail order bride with a fishy secret... Crabs with a collective consciousness... A vampire who transforms into a Candiru... Zombie piranha...Bait that will have you crawling out of your skin and more. Drawing on horror, humor with a helping of dark fantasy and a touch of deviance, these 19 contemporary stories pay homage to the monsters that lurk in the murky waters of our imaginations. If you thought it was safe to go back in the water... Think Again!

Check out other great

Sea Monster Novels!

Michael Cole

SCAR

Scar is a killing machine. Born from DNA spliced between the extinct Megalodon and modern day Great White, he has a viciousness that transcends time. His evil is reflected in his eyes, his savagery in his two-inch serrated teeth, his ruthlessness in his trail of death. After escaping captivity, the killer shark travels to the island community Cross Point, where prey is in abundance. With an insatiable appetite, heightened senses, and skin impervious to bullets, Scar kills everything that crosses his path. His reign of terror puts him at war with the island sheriff, Nick Piatt. With the body count rising, Nick vows to protect his island community from the vicious threat. With the aid of a marine biologist, a rookie deputy, and a bad-tempered fisherman, Nick leads a crusade against Scar, as well as the ruthless scientist who created him.

Rick Chesler

HOTEL MEGALODON

An underwater luxury hotel on a gorgeous tropical island is set for an extravagant opening weekend with the world watching. The only thing standing in the way of a first-rate experience for the jet-setting VIPs is an unscrupulous businessman and sixty feet of prehistoric shark. As the underwater complex is besieged by a marauding behemoth, newly minted marine biologist Coco Keahi must face off against the ancient predator as it rises from the deep with a vengeance. Meanwhile, a human monster has decided he would be better off if Coco were one of the creature's victims.

www.ingramcontent.com/pod-product-compliance
Lightning Source LLC
Chambersburg PA
CBHW072241190626
46809CB00018B/2893

* 9 7 8 1 9 2 2 8 6 1 2 3 8 *